Kate Walker

THE SICILIAN'S WIFE

ITALIAN HUSBANDS

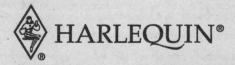

HARLEQUIN®

TORONTO • NEW YORK • LONDON
AMSTERDAM • PARIS • SYDNEY • HAMBURG
STOCKHOLM • ATHENS • TOKYO • MILAN • MADRID
PRAGUE • WARSAW • BUDAPEST • AUCKLAND

ISBN 0-373-12339-6

THE SICILIAN'S WIFE

First North American Publication 2003.

This edition published by arrangement with Harlequin Books S.A.

® and TM are trademarks of the publisher. Trademarks indicated with ® are registered in the United States Patent and Trademark Office, the Canadian Trade Marks Office and in other countries.

Visit us at www.eHarlequin.com

Printed in U.S.A.

"If that was all I ever wanted I could have asked a dozen women—more—to marry me over the years, but I did not."

"Why didn't you ask them?" she managed, knowing that it was what he wanted her to say. Cesare's smile was slow, almost benign, but there was something in his eyes that stopped it from being the tender response it appeared.

"They didn't offer me what I wanted," he said with a deliberate softness.

"And that was…?" she whispered, and watched his smile grow into a wicked grin.

"This…"

She barely had time to catch her breath before his mouth came down on hers, but it was with an unexpected gentleness that seemed to draw out her soul, take it away from her and hold it captive. And in that moment she knew that she was lost. Knew that no matter how hard she tried to convince herself, there was no way in the world that she was over Cesare Santorino.

CHAPTER ONE

TONIGHT he was going to ask her.

The words were clear and definite inside Cesare's head, voicing the resolve he had held to for years now.

He had been waiting for this day for ever it seemed. Six long years. Too long. It had been a wait that had tried all his patience, straining it to breaking point at times. But tonight the waiting had come to an end. Tonight Megan was going to be his.

The sound of the doorbell ringing through the house jolted him slightly, making him grimace wryly as he snatched his finger off hastily. He was risking sounding more like the police arriving with a warrant for someone's arrest rather than a would-be lover who had waited longer then he could bear for the woman he wanted more than any other.

'Mr Santorino!'

The housekeeper sounded flustered and confused as well she might, Cesare reflected ruefully. Normally his visits were well prepared for, notice given of his arrival long in advance. He was an honoured guest in this house, welcomed as a friend as well as a business colleague, so his arrival like this was not only out of the blue, it was also totally out of character.

'We weren't expecting you. Mr Ellis didn't say...'

'No...'

One lean brown hand came up to cut off her words, brushing aside her nervously apologetic explanation.

'He would not have said, because he didn't know. I

didn't tell him I was coming to England, or that I was likely to call.'

'But...'

Mrs Moore took a small step backwards, obviously feeling that she should invite him in, then hesitated again.

'I'm afraid Mr Ellis isn't here. He's visiting relatives in Scotland. There's only Miss Megan...'

'Ah, so Megan is home, is she?'

He was pleased with the tone he managed to use; glad to hear that he sounded both disinterested and faintly surprised. Hearing him, no one would have thought that his visit here tonight had been calculated for just this effect. That he had come to England knowing that Tom was away, and that his only daughter was in the house on her own.

'I take it she's back from university now then is she?'

'That's right. Finished her degree and everything. She got back at the weekend—on her own, surprisingly.'

'On her own?'

No. That question had been too sharp, betraying too much of an interest and a degree of shock than was wise.

'Yes, I thought she'd bring the boyfriend with her.'

Belatedly, the housekeeper realised that keeping her employer's friend standing on the doorstep was not the most polite approach. Mrs Moore moved further back into the wide, tiled hallway.

'Won't you come inside, sir? I'm sure Miss Megan would be delighted to see you.'

Privately, Cesare took the liberty of doubting that she would be any such thing. The way he and Megan had parted the last time he had seen her, at a New Year party given by her father, he had little hope that 'delighted' would describe her reaction to him now. When he had resolved on this visit, he had had every confidence that he could soon overcome any initial resistance, but the mention of a boyfriend was an unexpected complication, one he should have forseen but, foolishly, had not.

'I'll tell her you're here...'

'*No!*'

Idiota! He reproved himself inwardly at the realisation that once again he had almost given himself away. That '*No*' had been too quick, the lapse into his native Italian giving too much away.

Hastily he switched on a covering smile, fixing his deep brown eyes on the housekeeper's face. It was a calculated move, one that had melted far harder hearts than hers in the past, and it had exactly the effect he wanted now.

'Don't announce me. I'd like to do it myself—give her a surprise.'

'Of course. She's in the library.'

Mrs Moore waved a hand in the direction of a door at the far end of the hall.

'I'm sure she'll be glad to see you. If you want my opinion she's a little run down at the moment—far too pale and thin for my liking. She's probably been burning the candle at both ends and not eating properly.'

'Probably.'

It was a struggle to contain his impatience. Would the woman never go?

At last she seemed to realise that he was anxious to move and turned in the direction of the kitchen. But then just as Cesare felt some of the tension that held his muscles taut start to ease she hesitated and turned back again.

'Should I bring in some coffee? A cold drink?'

'I'll ring if we need anything.'

It was the tone he adopted with difficult employees. One that demanded instant, unquestioning obedience—and always got it. It worked this time too. The housekeeper nodded, made a small, awkward movement, almost as if she was coming close to bobbing a respectful curtsey, then turned and trotted away, her heels clicking in the silent hall.

At last!

Cesare gave a deep sigh of relief as he pushed both his hands through his jet-black hair. It was almost as if the housekeeper had sensed his intent, the reason why he was here tonight, and had set herself up as the moral guardian of the daughter of the house, the defender of Megan's honour, against the dark intrusive force of a sexually mature male.

His beautifully curved mouth twisted slightly cynically as he shut the door quietly. He didn't want to alert Megan to his presence. Wanted to come up on her unawares. And it wasn't her honour he wanted to steal. It was her heart.

Megan had heard the doorbell some time earlier but had decided to ignore it. If it was important then Mrs Moore would come and fetch her. If it wasn't, then the housekeeper could deal with it. The older woman knew much more about her father's daily life than she did since she had been away at university. And besides, she wasn't in the mood for company.

'What am I going to do?'

Sighing, she pushed aside the sleek fall of her auburn hair and propped her chin on her hands, elbows resting on the table at which she sat. A book lay open in front of her, one she had been making a pretence at reading. But it had been simply for something to do, and her mossy-green eyes had been left so unfocused by tears that the words on the pages danced in front of her vision in a totally incomprehensible blur.

'What *am* I going to do?'

She had asked the question of herself again and again more times than she cared to remember, but there had never been a hope of an answer in her mind. She didn't know what to do, or where to turn next.

'Megan?'

The sound of the door opening jolted her head up, but it was the figure who appeared in the doorway, tall, dark and devastating that had her blinking in stunned disbelief, unable to believe that she was seeing correctly.

'Cesare?'

Her heart gave one violent, breath-snatching thud against her ribcage, leaving her gasping in shock. Cesare Santorino was the last person she had expected to see here tonight. The last person she *wanted* to see as well.

But that didn't stop her foolish emotions going into overdrive simply to see him.

She had once adored every inch of this man's tall, rangy body, dreamed of losing herself in his arms, of drowning in the deep, molten bronze of his eyes. The image of his forcefully carved features had etched itself into her memory, so that for many nights the last thought in her mind as she drifted asleep had been of the slash of high, slanting cheekbones, the shockingly sensual curve of his wide mouth, the hard strength of his jaw and chin.

'What are you doing here?'

To her annoyance, her voice came and went like a badly tuned radio and she had to fight to get it under control. It was just the way she was feeling, she told herself angrily. Just the low mood that had already affected her so badly. Nothing more.

She was *over* Cesare, had been over him for months; ever since that disastrous party at New Year when he had humiliated her so badly. Before then she had worshipped the ground he walked on, but that night he had taken her devotion, her pride, and trampled it underneath his beautifully polished, handmade leather shoes.

'If you want to see my dad, then he's not here...'

'I know,' Cesare cut in sharply, a faint frown drawing his dark straight brows together. 'It was you I came to see.'

'Me?'

That frown, and something in the intonation of his lyrically accented voice set her nerves on edge, raising the tiny hairs on the back of her neck in wary apprehension. She was suddenly painfully aware of the blurred marks of tears on her cheeks, only roughly scrubbed away with the back of her hand.

'What did you want me for?'

She got to her feet as she spoke, moving away from the direct light of the window, into a more shadowy part of the room.

'I didn't think you ever wanted to speak to me again.'

'Why ever not?' Infuriatingly it was touched with a thread of amusement that scraped over her skin.

'You made it plain that you didn't want to waste your time with me.'

His slow, sexy smile did terrible things to what little composure she had left, making her feel as if a powerful cord was tightening around her heart and tugging hard.

'Oh, Megan, *cara*, you weren't in any fit state to spend time with anyone—waste or not.'

'I'd had a glass or two of champagne!'

But what she was never going to admit was that it had not been the sparkling wine that had intoxicated her, but the sheer impact of his presence, lethally elegant and stunning in the stark black and white of traditional evening wear.

'Or three, or four...' Cesare returned drily. 'And the problem was that you were hellishly enticing in your tiddly state. Do you have any idea just how sweetly seductive you looked in that slip of a dress?'

'Sweetly...' Megan echoed, totally bemused.

Had he really said what she thought he had said? Had he really used the words *enticing* and *seductive* to describe her? Even through the haze of misery that clouded her thoughts, the words touched something in her. Something that she had believed was long since dead. Something that still lingered in the heart she was sure she had armoured against him after that last, humiliating, public rejection of her.

'You're kidding!'

'Not at all.'

Cesare shook his dark head, moving at last, strolling into the room with the lithe ease of a hunting cat, letting the door swing to silently behind him.

'It was all that I could do to keep my hands off you.'

The only response that Megan could manage was a loud, unladylike snort, vividly expressing her cynical opinion of that comment.

'Oh sure! You had such a struggle that you put me aside as if just touching me might contaminate you. And then you...then you ignored me for the rest of the night. No?'

She blinked in confusion as Cesare shook his dark head.

'No,' he stated flatly. 'There was no way I could ignore you, no matter how I tried. I've never been able to ignore you. Not from the moment you bounced into my life as a pretty thirteen-year-old, the first time I ever visited this house. I couldn't take my eyes off you then, and I've never been able to since.'

He still couldn't. If she was in a room, there was only one direction in which his eyes would be drawn. She was like some vivid, bright spark, burning so brilliantly that it almost blinded him. And the hardest thing had been that he could never admit to it; never reveal the way he felt.

Until now.

And she was so much more lovely now; the beauty that had promised as an adolescent becoming reality in the young woman who stood before him. She had hair like the burnished leaves of a copper beech tree, eyes like the deepest, mossy pools above the finest cheekbones he had ever seen. Tall and slender, she was curved in all the right places that declared her femininity, and her skin had the smooth softness of a peach so that his fingers itched to touch it.

But he had given his promise to her father, and had sworn to abide by it until the date of her twenty-second birthday set him free.

'You're kidding!'

'I would never joke about something like this.'

'Cesare...'

Megan shook her head in bemusement. This couldn't be happening! Nothing he was saying seemed as if it could possibly be true. And the worst, the bitterest irony, was that these words were the ones she had always dreamed of hearing him say. Dreamed, but known that those dreams would never become reality.

She had had the world's greatest crush on this man since she had been in her teens. But he was eight years older than her, a sophisticated, cosmopolitan businessman, the owner of the huge corporation of which her father's firm was just one microscopic, unimportant component. Men like Cesare Santorino didn't take any notice of girls like her.

'Stop messing—don't tease me like this.'

'What makes you think that I'm teasing?'

Looking into his dark, inscrutable face, she could almost believe that he meant it. There was no trace of amusement in those burning eyes, no hint of a smile on the sensual mouth.

'But you have to be...'

Again his proud head moved in denial of her protest.

'No, *cara*. There is no "have to be" about this. I am telling the absolute truth.'

'You can't be...'

All the strength went from her legs and she dropped down into the nearest chair, unable to keep upright any longer. And at least this way she could put some distance between them.

'I don't believe you!'

'Believe it!'

Oh, this was worse than ever! Bending down, he had placed both strong-fingered hands on the arms of the chair, one on either side of her. Imprisoned in the cage made by them and his powerful body, the wall of his chest in the immaculate white shirt a solid barrier between her and escape, she could look nowhere but into the smouldering bronze of his eyes.

And suddenly she was reminded of the volcano Etna on his native island of Sicily. The burn of his eyes made her think of the molten lava that had poured down the mountain's sides, scorching everything in its path. She felt as if his gaze had just the same heated power, searing over the delicacy of the exposed skin of her face and neck.

He was so close that she could smell the clean scent of his body, mixed with the tang of some citrus cologne, light and invigorating—and painfully stimulating to her already overwrought nerves. Her heart was thudding in double-quick time, her breath coming raw and uneven.

'Don't do this to me! Not now! What is this, Cesare—some sort of twisted little game? Do you get some fun out of tormenting me, lying to me? Because—'

'Would it help if I swore I am not lying now—but that I had lied in the past?'

'Lied?'

It seemed that with every word he spoke the situation got stranger and stranger, more complicated and tangled, impossible to sort out. It was as if the Cesare Santorino that she had thought she knew had been taken away and someone new and totally alien had been put in his place.

'When did you lie to me?'

Her mouth had dried painfully and the words came out on an embarrassing croak.

'When I said I wasn't interested in you. When I acted as if you bored me. When I—'

'No—stop it—no, no, *no*!'

Megan flung her hands up to cover her ears and then rapidly moved them so that they covered her face.

'Stop it!' she muttered into the protection of her concealing fingers. 'This isn't fair!'

This time last year—on her twenty-first birthday—she would have been overjoyed to hear those words. At Christmas, and even more at that dreadful New Year party, they would have set her heart dancing for joy, made her spirits sing. But now it was too late.

Then she couldn't think of anything that could have been better. Now she couldn't think of anything *worse*. Because if anything Cesare claimed was the truth in any way, then it very soon wouldn't be when he found out...

'Stop it!' she repeated more fiercely this time.

'*Mi dispiace*—I am sorry.'

He'd moved too fast, Cesare told himself reproachfully. Impatience had always been a fault of his and this time he'd rushed right in when he would have done so much better to take things slowly.

He had promised himself he would take things slowly. But in the moment that he'd walked into the library and seen Megan in the flesh for the first time in over six months all his control had deserted him. He had struggled to hold on to that control for over six years now, and he hadn't been able to do so any longer.

'Forgive me Megan...'

His tone was so rough, so unbelievably raw with some emotion that it forced Megan to lower her protective hands, gazing up at him in shock and bewilderment.

And that bewilderment struck at Cesare like a reproach.

'Forgive me...' he said again, lifting his hands swiftly from the chair arms and flinging them up and out in a supremely Italian gesture of surrender.

'You are right. I was in the wrong to tease you—wrong and cruel. I should never have done it.'

It was only what she had expected, Megan told herself dully as she watched him swing away from her and prowl moodily across the wide, polished wooden floor, his shoulders hunched, hands pushed deep into the pockets of his trousers. She had known all along that he wasn't telling the truth. That he was just tormenting her as he had done when she was little more than a child, and he had been a sophisticated twenty-two year old.

Then he had mocked her starry-eyed hero-worship of him playing on it mercilessly to have her fetching and carrying for him, taking advantage of her keenness to perform any tiny task she could for the object of her devotion. And now it seemed that he was doing it again.

It was only what she had expected but, right now, with the worry that was always there, just below the surface of her mind, nagging at her and throwing her into total confusion about what she should do, his teasing seemed so much worse.

It *hurt*. It hurt terribly, adding another layer to the pain of the way Gary had behaved, and the consequences of that behaviour until her head swum sickeningly, and she was unable to think straight.

'It's all right,' she managed stiffly. 'After all, it's only what I'd expect from you. But now that you've had your fun, would you mind leaving?'

With an effort she brought her chin up, forced her green eyes to meet his dark gaze defiantly.

'I'd prefer to be alone.'

'Fun?'

He didn't seem to have heard the last comment or, if he had, he was deliberately ignoring it.

'*Fun*!'

Shock roughed his voice, stopped his restless prowling.

'You think that this is just *un divertimento*? That I am playing with you?'

'Well, isn't it?' Her chin lifted a little higher. 'What else could it be?' she challenged.

'*La verita*!' Cesare shot back, his tone like the crack of a gun. 'The truth!'

'The *truth*! Oh come on! Don't…don't…'

To her horror, her voice began to tremble, so that she stumbled over the words she wanted. It was too much. Too cruel. He'd taken his joke too far. And she was in no fit state to be able to cope with this new, sophisticated form of emotional torture.

'Don't do this to me!' she wailed, her voice high and tight.

The pain in her words was like a blow to his face, making him freeze into stillness, eyes narrowing sharply. Something was very wrong here. Something much more than any distress at his heavy-handed teasing.

'What is it?' he asked. 'What's wrong?'

And then, when she could only shake her head in mute, numb misery, he came close—closer—one warm strong hand sliding under her chin and lifting her face to meet his brown-eyed scrutiny.

Her cheeks were wet with tears. Tears that had trickled down her face, dripping off her chin. And more were welling up inside her eyes, making the deep green glisten like polished gemstones.

'*Carina*, why are you crying? Meggie…'

Unthinkingly, the word slid past his lips, using the long ago nickname she had had as a child.

'Tell me what's wrong.'

It was the name that did it. If he hadn't said 'Meggie…' in quite that way. If he hadn't used that once familiar, now rarely spoken, nickname, the name only those closest and dearest to her had used in the past, then she might have been able to resist it.

But he had said 'Meggie,' and both his voice and his expression had softened on the word. Just for a moment he had pushed aside time and had taken her back to the days when life had been sweet, idyllic, uncomplicated. The perfect bliss of a summer when the sun had always seemed to be shining, and nothing could possibly go wrong.

Days when she had still held on to a dream that one day this man would love her. That somewhere, stretching ahead of her, lay a bright and wonderful future, filled with happy ever after. A future that now was totally beyond her reach.

And suddenly she knew, totally and irredeemably, without a hope of any other possibility, that she was going to tell him the whole sorry story.

CHAPTER TWO

'MEGGIE—*tell me*!'

This time, Cesare's use of the childish nickname was far from gentle. Her hesitation, the seconds she had spent hunting for the right words to tell him what was on her mind, had pushed him to the limits of his patience in a very short space of time. He was barely keeping hold of his tenuous grip on his temper, and the way the words hissed through his teeth made that plain.

'Just what is the problem? I need to know.'

It was the impatience in his tone that caught on Megan's tongue and held it immobile, unable to speak a word. That and the way that, towering over her, big, dark and dangerously imposing, a severe frown drawing together the black arcs of his brows, Cesare had reverted to the man she had known—and feared—as an adolescent. Then he had been able to strike her dumb simply by walking into a room, and any attempt to answer one of the occasional questions he arrogantly tossed her way had reduced her to a mumbling, stammering, red-faced heap of embarrassment totally unlike her normally reasonable, sensibly functioning self.

And that was just what he did to her now.

'Megan...'

This time her name had a note of warning in it. One that only made matters so much worse. She could only shake her head despairingly, unable to find any words with which to answer him.

'Is it your father? Are you worried about the problems he's having with the company?'

'He told you about that?' Shock released her tongue, pushed the words from her mouth.

'Of course he told me—I am a friend after all.'

'Did he ask you to help him—to bail him out? And you agreed?'

Some degree of strength was returning to her limbs now, and her brain seemed to be functioning with just a degree or two of clarity. If he was prepared to help her father, save Tom Ellis from the almost inevitable bankruptcy that was now staring him in the face, then at least one of her worries would be eased.

'You said you'll lend him what he needs?'

The change in Cesare's face gave her the answer without a word having been spoken. The dark, carved features seemed to close up; the burnt-coffee-coloured eyes clouding as they met the urgent entreaty in hers. He had moved away from her mentally before he stepped back physically, withdrawing into himself in the space of a couple of heartbeats.

'No,' he said softly. 'I did not.'

'You did not!' Megan repeated, unable to believe what she had heard. 'You said *no*! I don't believe—'

'Believe it!' Cesare cut in sharply, not liking this direction the conversation had taken. 'Your father told me of his problems. Regrettably...'

'Regrettably... Oh, yes, I just bet you *regretted* it.'

The cynicism in Megan's voice, the way it twisted at her mouth, dulled her eyes, made him wince. He wouldn't have hurt her this way if he could have helped it.

'You could have afforded it! The amount he needed would have been just a drop in the ocean compared with the fortune you possess! Why, you must make that much or more in just a year or so!'

Megan had got to her feet now and was coming towards him furiously. The anger that sparked in the depths of her eyes actually made him take a step or two backwards, away from her.

'Yes, I could have afforded it.'

'And you weren't prepared to do so! I thought you were his *friend*!'

'I am. *Dannazione*, Megan, you know I am!'

The haughty toss of her head dismissed his words with supreme contempt, green flames flaring in the angry eyes that blazed into his.

'Some sort of friend that wouldn't help him when he most needed you!'

Cesare could not hold back an impatient sigh as he raked both hands through the midnight-dark strands of his hair. He had hoped to have this conversation later—much, much later when things would have had a very different sort of perspective.

'Meggie,' he remonstrated as calmly as possible, 'it wouldn't have done any good. Your father understands that.'

'Well, I don't! I think you're going to have to explain it for those of us who aren't blessed with your near-genius financial ability. And don't "Meggie" me! I might have let you call me that when I was growing up, but I'm no longer a child. I'm a woman of twenty-two, with three years at university and a degree behind me. I've done a lot of maturing lately!'

'You certainly have.'

Dark-chocolate eyes skimmed over her slender figure in the close-fitting jeans and T-shirt, lingering appreciatively on the high curves of her breasts in a way that made Megan think unwillingly of the changes she had sensed in her body over the last week or so.

'My name is Megan and I'll thank you to remember that!'

'Of course.'

His smile at her outrage was wry, and the small, side-ways inclination of his head in acknowledgement of her outburst seemed to make a mockery of the apparent gesture of submission.

'Are you laughing at me?' Megan demanded suspiciously.

'Would I dare?' he returned drily, the lift of humour in his voice, the hint of a gleam in his eyes, tugging at something in her heart.

The man was too damned attractive for his own good, she told herself furiously—furiously because she didn't want to find anything in him appealing right now. Once she had thought him the most delicious, the most devastating man in the world, but not any more. Especially not now! Though when he smiled like that...

Hastily she caught herself up, cursing her wandering mind. Such thoughts were dangerous, weakening her when she most needed to be strong.

'My father might understand, but I certainly don't! Would you care to explain?'

No, Cesare answered in the privacy of his thoughts. No, I would definitely not care to explain. Once more he was caught by the way he had given his word to Tom Ellis. The older man was proud to the point of stupidity. Even to rescue his company he couldn't take a hand-out from his friend—but his *son-in-law* was a different matter.

'If Meggie marries you,' he'd said, 'then I'll take your money. It will be a family matter then. But not otherwise.'

Tom had demanded that this deal was to be a secret between the two of them and, knowing it was the only way his stubborn friend would take his help, he had been forced to agree. But his loyalty to Tom was being worn away by his feelings for the woman in front of him.

Did she know how it twisted a knife in his heart when she had looked at him, first with that entreaty in her eyes, and then with the scorn that had replaced it? And what made it so much worse was the instinctive, very basic way that his body reacted simply to being in the same room as her. Every sense was on heated red-alert, his pulse throbbing heavily in his veins. Since the moment he had walked into the room to find her sitting in the shadows, he had been fighting the impulse to grab her and kiss her, plundering her mouth with the force of the hunger that had him in its grip.

But to act on that impulse would be the most stupid behaviour he could come up with. At best, it would annoy and alienate her. At worst, it would drive her right away from him, send her screaming from the room. With a violent struggle he pushed the uncomfortable feelings back down inside himself, stamping on them hard.

'Cesare...' Megan's tone was a warning. 'Explain!'

'Your father's in a very tricky situation,' he began carefully. 'The state of the markets has just about destroyed the value of his investments—and the company's been having problems too.'

'So why wouldn't you help him?'

'I'm not in the business of buying up failing concerns! If word got about that I'd done it for one, then next moment I'd have thousands of lame dogs at my door, looking for a rescue deal—a hand-out!'

Pushed to the limit by the reproach in her voice, Cesare flung the words at her then almost immediately wished them back as he saw her recoil in distaste at his outburst. For perhaps the millionth time he cursed the promises to Tom Ellis that tied him down, making him feel like an angry, frustrated fly caught in the imprisoning, sticky threads of a huge spider's web.

'It isn't sound business sense, Megan.' But for Tom he would do it. If he got the chance.

'Oh, and we must always put "business sense" first!' Megan flung back bitterly.

'I wouldn't have got where I am unless I had.'

'No—you wouldn't. But now that you are where you are, you seem to have lost all sense of caring about the smaller man. You used to have more charity than this, Cesare!'

'It wouldn't help!'

Stung beyond endurance, Cesare couldn't hold back any longer. His conscience only added to the feeling of mental discomfort, giving him another reproachful twist as he saw her flinch as if he had slapped her in the face.

'Your father's in too deep—and he knows it! He couldn't manage another loan—he owes too much already to too many people.'

Her silence betrayed the depth of her shock, and his spirits, already low, sank right to rock-bottom. This wasn't how this had been supposed to go. But from the moment he had walked into the library nothing had followed the path he had expected.

'It—it's that bad?'

Megan felt as if there were a thousand angrily buzzing bees swarming inside her head, making it swim unpleasantly so that rational thought was impossible.

'Cesare—are you telling me that—he's ruined?'

He didn't have to spell it out. It was there in his face, etching lines around the stunning eyes, the beautiful mouth.

'Oh, no!'

Her legs went from under her, threatening to send her crashing to the floor but, even as she sagged weakly, Cesare had moved, coming to her side with the swift, instinctive reflex action of a hunting tiger. Powerful arms folded round her, enclosing and supporting her, holding her close as one hand fluttered in a weak gesture of supplication.

'It's all right, *carina*.' His voice was rough, sounding husky in her ear. 'I have you safe. I won't let you fall.'

Safe, Megan thought hazily, the single word, the only one that would register in her clouded thoughts. Yes, here, at last, she felt safe. For the first time in six long, unhappy weeks, she felt something other than lost and afraid and alone. It seemed as if Cesare's strength flowed along his arms and into her through the strong-fingered hands that clasped her around her waist.

The heat of his body surrounded her, the clean, musky scent of his skin reaching her nostrils, making her want to inhale deeply, as if to draw in more of him that way. The urge to lean on him even more was irresistible, her head feeling too heavy for her neck to support. Giving in to the impulse, she let her head drop down onto his shoulder, feeling the hard bone, the taut muscle provide the perfect, much needed rest.

'Oh, Cesare…' she sighed, abandoning herself to the luxury of giving in to a moment of weakness.

'Megan…'

His voice was unexpectedly gruff and tight. Her heart thudded in time with his breathing, the sound of his own pulse under her cheek providing an echo, beat for beat. Again Megan sighed, nestling closer, turning her head so that her mouth was close to the smooth, bronzed skin of his neck.

'Megan…'

This time there was a note of what seemed like warning in his use of her name, but she was too comfortable, too relaxed to heed it. For the first time since she had left Lancaster and travelled back to London at the end of her university life, she felt as if she had truly come home. As if she was where she wanted to be. Where she had always been meant to be.

The heavy throb of Cesare's heart gave a sudden jolt then lurched into a new and faster beat and she felt her own pulse quicken in response. Her breathing became faster too, shallower, uneven, until it was rasping in and out of her lungs like liquid fire.

'Cesare...'

She tried for his name but the heat inside her had dried her throat so that the single word came out on a raw, uneven croak. Her lips were parched and as she licked them nervously to ease the uncomfortable sensation she felt the faint adjustment of his head, knew even before she opened her eyes that he was looking down at her and that he had caught the small, betraying movement.

Her eyelids felt unnaturally heavy and swollen so that it was an effort to lift them and meet his gaze. But in the second that she managed it and looked straight into the dark unblinking force of his stare, she was caught and held transfixed, like a rabbit in the oncoming glare of a car's headlights.

And she didn't want to move. Instead she waited, outwardly patient, but inwardly fizzing with anticipation and excitement. Waited, knowing that this was a moment she had been moving towards all her life. One that she had dreamed would come, then feared she had missed out on altogether, but which now she knew was as inevitable as her next breath, the beat of her heart.

'Megan...' Cesare began again in a voice that was thick and raw and sounded quite unlike the controlled, sophisticated man she had always known. 'I think I'm going to have to kiss you.'

'I know...'

'I am sorry if you—you *know*?'

'Mmm.'

Megan nodded slightly, feeling the brush of the soft cotton of his shirt against her cheek, the warmth of his skin burning through it.

'I know. And do you know something?'

Her mouth quirked up at the corners into a mischievous pixie-like smile.

'I'm going to have to let you—'

The words were smothered, crushed back down her throat, as his mouth covered hers. With a rough, jerky movement, he swung her round in front of him, his hands coming up to the back of her head, shaping themselves round the fine bones of her skull, holding her close, crushing her face up against his. It was the wildest, most passionate kiss of her life, one that drove her breath away, made her head spin, set her heart pounding.

Her own arms went up around his neck, fingers twisting and tangling in the black silk of his hair, keeping him still when he would have moved away. Her whole body was suffused with a heat that was more primitive, more basic, more pagan, than the simple effect of feeling the hard, hot length of him against her. She was on fire with delight, with hunger, with need, her hands moving lower, clutching, clinging, stroking. She was unable to get enough of him, unable to touch enough of him all at once.

'*Madre di Dio!*' Cesare muttered against her lips, snatching in a quick, raw breath as best he could without actually moving away. 'Oh, Megan, Megan...'

'Did you know, I love the way you say my name?'

Megan's response was breathless too, shaking on an edge of near-laughter.

'*Maygan...Maygan,*' she echoed his pronunciation deliberately. 'It sounds something special, something much more exotic and sensual than plain, ordinary Megan Ellis could ever be.'

'No! Never say that.'

Cesare shook his dark head in reproof, laying one long finger across her lips to silence her.

'Never say the words plain and ordinary in the same sentence as your name. The two things should never be linked together. You are not plain—and you are most definitely not ordinary!'

'No?'

Megan looked up at him in stunned bewilderment, hunting for the teasing, the amusement she felt sure must be gleaming in his eyes. She didn't find it. Instead she saw a very different sort of light burning in the brown depths. The sort of glow that made her think of fires and heat and the scorching, searing heat of the sun. Her heart gave a sudden, jolting shudder of excitement inside her chest, so that she gasped aloud in shock.

'You're beautiful—*squisita*—a stunning, wonderful woman.'

'*Squi—squisita*—exquisite!'

Megan couldn't believe what she was hearing. She felt like a child who had been caught with her nose pressed up against the window of a sweetshop, only to have the owner come to the door and invite her in to help herself to anything and everything she wanted.

'You're—you have to be joking! No?' she questioned, silenced once more by the rough, shake of his head.

'No joke,' he insisted in a tone that made it plain she shouldn't allow herself even to begin to doubt that he was deadly serious. 'Would I joke about something like this?'

One hand trailed softly down her hair, smoothing and caressing the bright auburn strands, lifting them and letting them coil softly around his fingers.

'About hair that burns like the glow of lava from a volcano in the dead of night...'

To her astonishment he bent his head and pressed his lips to the strand of hair in his hand, kissing it softly.

'Eyes that have the cool, shadowy appeal of the olive groves...'

He repeated the caress, this time on her eyes, pressing her lids shut with the soft pressure of his mouth and lingering there for a moment that held her entranced, her heart seeming to stop, her breathing become so shallow it was almost non-existent.

'Skin so soft and so delicate I'm almost afraid to touch it for fear it would bruise like a ripe peach...'

For a second the blunt tips of his fingers hovered over her face before gliding softly downwards, tracing the line of her cheek, her jaw, with a delicacy that made her shiver in uncontrolled response. But when his lips followed the same path then she froze in sensual delight, keeping her eyes tight shut in order to better enjoy the exquisite sensations he was creating.

Cesare's mouth moved over her skin, kissing, caressing, occasionally nipping very softly, until it reached her lips and covered them again.

'And a mouth,' he murmured against them, 'that is just made for kissing.'

This time his kiss was pure sensual enticement, the sort of kiss that seemed to draw her soul out of her body, making her head swim and her blood heat in her veins.

She melted against him, her body arcing as it pressed up against his, her breath catching in her throat as she felt the heated, swollen evidence of the reality of his desire for her. He might be able to choose his words, disguise his tone in order to be able to carry out whatever tormenting plan had been in his mind, if he had meant to tease her as he had done in the past. But this was no tease. This was hard, solid, physical reality. The uncontrollable response of a man to a woman for whom he felt a desire that he was incapable of concealing.

And the same response was flooding through her own body, melting her already vulnerable heart, twisting along her nerves. Every sense throbbed in hungry reaction, sending a stinging sensation straight to the most intimate, most feminine point between her legs. Sighing her need into his mouth, Megan moved restlessly, her hands clutching at the broad strength of his shoulders as the unwary movement brought her once more up against the heat and force of his erection.

'I think we would be a little more comfortable if we...'

The rest of Cesare's words were lost in another long, burning kiss, but Megan didn't need words. Half-blind, totally absorbed, she would have followed him anywhere, and so she went with him, step by sightless step as he led her towards the big, squashy settee that stood before the huge open fireplace in the centre of the library.

'Sit down...' he dragged his mouth from hers long enough to say.

Obediently she sank down onto the soft cushions, her clinging hands pulling him down with her. As soon as he was beside her she moved closer, taking his mouth for herself, letting her tongue play intimately with his and slide along his lips.

'Meggie...'

This time she found nothing to object to in his use of her childhood name. It was soft and tender, a seductive and a verbal caress in one. But what excited her most was the thread of total surrender in the sound, the wordless declaration of the way that he had abandoned himself totally to her lead.

The thought gave her a thrilling sense of power, one that had her reaching for his tie and tugging it loose at his throat. No sooner had she exposed the tanned skin, the strong, corded lines of his neck than the overwhelming need for more gripped her, driving her to impulsive action. Leaning forward, she pressed her lips against the point where his pulse raced, hard and strong, savouring the slightly salty taste of his flesh, the heated velvet against her mouth.

'*Meggie!*'

It was a groan of resignation, a sound of total abandonment. In one twisting movement he came to lie on his back on the wide settee, with Megan half at his side, half lying across the supporting strength of his body.

His hands were impatient now, tugging the white T-shirt free of her jeans at her waist, pushing it upwards over her slender ribcage, his fingers caressing the exposed skin left in its path. Megan caught her breath sharply, writhing in pure delight, her breasts hardening, pouting, pushing against the confinement of her bra in a physical mirroring of the burning arousal she had seen in Cesare himself already.

'*Bellissima, magnifica, squisita...*' Cesare had lapsed into his own language, crooning the words deep in his throat, his lyrical accent growing deeper, more musical on every word. 'Megan, you always were enchanting as a child, but as a woman...'

Words failed him as he lifted passion-glazed eyes to hers and for a moment it seemed as if time had frozen. For long, silent seconds, their gazes locked and it seemed to Megan that in that time there was some wordless question asked, and equally soundlessly answered.

She thought she could guess what was in Cesare's mind. He still thought of her as a child, the infuriating youngster who had hung around him, dogging his every step until she must have driven him to distraction. And those thoughts must make him hesitate, wonder if she was ready to go further, if she was woman enough for him.

Surely the fearless, unwavering way she met that burning, questioning stare was enough of an answer for him? But just in case it wasn't, she lowered her head and took his mouth again, deliberately putting every ounce of sensuality and enticement she possessed into the kiss, using it to communicate the heated need that throbbed between her legs.

'The answer's yes, Cesare,' she whispered unevenly, her mouth very close to his ear. 'If you want me then yes, yes, *yes*! I'm yours right here and now—anywhere and anyway you want me!'

His only answer was a thickly muttered and near-incoherent curse in raw Italian and a moment later Megan too was beyond thought as hot fingers slid underneath the elastic sides of her bra, not even pausing to unfasten the slip of lace at the back. Her involuntary cry as the hard warmth of his palms cupped and held the soft weight of her breasts was a primitive sound of ecstasy, her head going back, her eyes staring sightlessly ahead. And when his thumbs moved, softly, slowly encircling her nipples in a tormenting, tantalising dance of provocation she writhed in delight under his touch, sighing her pleasure.

'*Madre de Dios*!'

Cesare muttered in Italian again, tugging off her clinging T-shirt and tossing it impatiently aside before coming back to take her breasts into his hands once more, holding them up and out so that all he had to do was lift his head ever so slightly from the worn velvet cushions and he could take one swollen tip into his mouth, suckling on it hard.

'Megan, *mia amante*, you weren't lying when you said

you'd done a lot of growing up lately. When I last saw you, you were still a little girl…'

A wickedly hot tongue snaked out, slid over the sensitised nipple, making her shudder violently in uncontrolled response.

'Here, as everywhere else. But you've changed, developed…become all woman.'

Changed. Developed. Become all woman. The words echoed bleakly inside Megan's head, becoming more frighteningly ominous with every repetition. And just the sound of them was a dreadful, hateful reminder, a violent death knell to all her hopes, dousing her passion in one brutal, bitterly cold rush.

'No!'

It was a cry of pain, of bewilderment, of confusion, sounding high and wild in the echoing room. And it froze Cesare into immediate stillness.

'No?'

It was like being slapped hard in the face. One moment she had been wild and willing, totally uninhibited in his arms. The next…

'You don't—you can't mean it!'

'I can! I don't want this!'

'Little liar.'

It was softly vicious, deadly. The nagging ache of frustrated passion was doing nothing at all to help his ability to think straight or reasonably.

'You're just teasing, you—'

'No! That's not it at all!'

With unexpected strength she tore herself from his restraining arms, flinging herself halfway across the polished floor towards the marble fireplace. Wrapping her arms around herself, concealing the creamy breasts his ardent passion had newly exposed, she shook her head so violently that her russet hair flew in a wild arc around her.

'You have to believe me! I'm not teasing—honestly I'm not! I don't want this!'

But that was too much.

'You "don't want",' Cesare echoed with gentle menace. 'You *"don't want"*! Oh, come now, *cara*, stop playing games! You were up for it every bit as much as I was— and don't try to deny it!' he snapped, seeing that she was about to refute the accusation once again. 'I'm not blind— or deaf! I could see the passion in your eyes—hear it in your voice. "If you want me then, *yes*!"'

Megan flinched as he quoted her own thoughtless words of only moments before, echoing her passionate tone with cruel accuracy.

'"I'm yours...anywhere and anyway you want me!" That *was* what you said, wasn't it?'

'Yes...'

Megan could only whisper words into the hands that concealed her ashen face.

'I know I said that but...'

But what? The question rang inside her head, self-reproach in every syllable.

'But I—I wasn't thinking straight.'

She couldn't have been thinking *at all* to let herself fall into Cesare's arms like that, to invite his kisses, caresses...*more*!

For a few crazy, deluded moments, she had let herself pretend that she was still the young, innocent Megan, the adolescent with the world's biggest ever crush on Cesare Santorino. And as that Megan she had seen his sudden new interest in her as the fulfilment of her long-held dream, the reward for half a lifetime of waiting.

But she was no longer that Megan. She no longer had

the freedom to indulge in such wild and wanton behaviour. She couldn't think only of herself…as Cesare's words had reminded her. And the thought of what might have been had brought with it such a bitter sense of loss that she felt as if someone had reached into her chest and ripped out her heart without hesitation.

'And it doesn't matter what I said because I can't—I can't…'

'Can't what?'

Cesare was sitting up now, dark eyes fixed on her, his breathing, and apparently his temper, at last under control. Only the way his skin was drawn tight over the forceful cheekbones betrayed the way he was feeling below the surface of apparent calm.

'Megan,' he began again when she could only shake her head weakly in mute despair. '*What* can't you do?'

'I can't sleep with you—or anyone. I mean, I can't have an affair with just anyone—no matter who.'

'And why not?'

But that was too much. She couldn't answer that question because she knew what his reaction would be. And right now she was feeling far too lost, too vulnerable to cope with the rejection that she knew he must inevitably toss in her direction when he knew the truth.

So she simply shook her head again, silent as before, fixing her unfocused eyes on the distant view from the window so as not to have to look into his dark, angry face.

'Megan—why not?'

Cesare's tone warned that he would not stop until he got an answer. She knew that he was totally ruthless when he was determined to get what he wanted. And he wanted to know the truth.

'Why can't you have an affair with me—or anyone?

Why? Megan—are you going to tell me, or do I have to
come over there and...'

The step he took towards her was positively the last
straw.

'All right!'

Megan cried out in despair and resignation.

'All right! I'll tell you! You want the truth—you can
have the truth!'

'And that is?' Cesare persisted mercilessly when she still
couldn't make herself form the words. 'Just what is the
truth that you...'

'That I'm pregnant!' Megan cut in when, having drawn
a deep, determined breath, she knew there was no going
back. 'That's what's happened. I had an affair at college—
I made a mistake and—and I'm pregnant as a result,' she
finished starkly. 'I'm having a baby in seven months' time.'

CHAPTER THREE

'YOU'RE *what*?'

If he had felt as if he had been slapped in the face earlier, then this sensation was painfully like being kicked somewhere much more delicate—and intimate. It worked like magic on the ache of his libido however, making it vanish in a trice, leaving him numbed and bewildered, his head spinning wildly.

'What did you say?'

He didn't need her to repeat the words; they were already disturbingly clear, etched into his thoughts in letters of fire. But he had to say something—*anything* at all. He had to keep talking—the most inane nonsense if necessary—just so he *didn't* say the things that were buzzing in his mind.

So he didn't say—what the hell did you go and do that for?

And he didn't shout. Though he wanted to. Didn't turn and kick something—anything. Though he wanted to. Didn't demand to know why she had given herself to someone else when she was *his*! Didn't she know that? Didn't she see that she had no *right* to be with anyone else—let alone sleep with anyone else? But he had spent so long—a lifetime it seemed, pretending with Megan. So somehow he just slipped back into how it had been.

And most of all, worst of all, he had to make sure that he never, ever, admitted to the raging inferno of jealousy that was surging through him. To the pain that was clawing at him, the blinding, black fury at the thought that she had cared for someone else enough to go to bed with him—to make love with him—to conceive a child with him.

'*What* did you say?' he repeated when Megan didn't speak, but simply stood, white-faced and huge-eyed, her bottom lip trembling slightly as she faced him.

'You know what I said! You heard me! I said that I'm pregnant.'

'And how, in the name of God, did that happen?'

Her smile, shaky though it was, was the last thing he had expected. Slightly wobbly and distinctly fraying at the edges, it was touched with a hint of wryness and just the tiniest bit of scepticism.

'Oh, Cesare, surely you of all people don't need to ask that! Don't you know about the birds and bees?'

'Yes, obviously I do,' he growled, uncomfortably. 'But you know what I mean. What happened?'

'I… Do you think you could pass me my T-shirt?' she said, changing the subject abruptly. 'I'm—I'd prefer to cover up, if you don't mind.'

If anything revealed the way that things had changed, the dramatic alteration in the atmosphere in the room, the way that the tension seemed to have drained away all the air so that it was impossible to breathe, then it was that simple phrase—'I'd *prefer* to cover up.' That and the way that she barely lifted a finger as she gestured in the direction of the white T-shirt still lying on the floor some feet away, where he had tossed it in the heat of passion.

There couldn't have been a greater contrast with the un-inhibited, wildly sexual siren who had delighted him on the settee just minutes before, and this uptight, heavily embarrassed woman who kept her arms firmly crossed over the lush curves of her breasts so as to keep herself hidden from him. She even managed to hook the T-shirt he tossed her on her thumb before determinedly turning her back in order to pull it on, concealing every sexy inch of herself from his watchful eyes.

But perhaps it was just as well, Cesare told himself, automatically smoothing down his ruffled hair and fastening the loosened buttons on his shirt with fingers that were not exactly steady. He needed to get himself back under control and think straight. And that was something he would never be fully capable of doing with a half-naked Megan standing in front of him.

So he waited, forcing himself to breathe slow and deep, until she was clothed again before deciding to speak once more.

'So,' he said when at last, dressed and apparently more composed, she slowly turned to face him. 'Are you going to tell me what happened?'

It was like being summoned to the headmaster's office to try and explain some kind of misdemeanour, Megan reflected, feeling reduced once more to the status of naughty schoolgirl, awaiting her punishment. No, it was worse than that. Cesare was counsel for the prosecution and judge and jury all rolled into one, the sombre, frowning disapproval on his face sending a sensation like the trickle of icy water running down her spine.

'You know what happened! You don't need me to tell you! I met this guy at a party—Gary. I—found him attractive and he made it plain he liked me. We started dating. One night our kisses led to more and more—as these things do…'

'As they do,' Cesare echoed in a voice that made her blood run cold. 'And so you ended up in bed together.'

'Do you have to make it sound so sordid!'

'It wasn't like that?'

The cynical lift of one jet-black brow almost destroyed her but she forced herself to ignore it and rushed on.

'No, it wasn't! It was nothing like that!'

'Ah, I see...'

Pushing his hands deep into his trouser pockets, Cesare leaned back against the velvet cushions and looked up at her through narrowed eyes. His coldly assessing stare was cruel as a laser, seeming to cut right through to her soul and lay it bare.

'You were madly in love with him?' His scepticism scraped over her skin, stripping away one protective layer.

'Yes! Yes I was!'

It was too vehement, too revealing. Especially to some-one who knew her as well as Cesare did. Surely he would be able to guess that she was protesting too much. That she was hiding behind a smokescreen of emotion?

She had thought she was in love with Gary. For a time she had truly believed it to be the case. But then circum-stances had changed, forcing her to reconsider. And if she hadn't already been doubting her own conviction, then her reaction to Cesare just now would have rubbed her nose forcibly in the uncomfortable truth.

'But he wasn't in love with you?'

Megan's bright head came up sharply, big green eyes becoming even bigger and darker.

'Why do you say that? How do you know?'

His indifferent shrug dismissed her question as the irrel-evant inanity it was.

'If he cared anything about you, he would be here now— with you. He wouldn't leave you to come home—face the music by yourself. I take it that was the reason for your tears?—Megan!' he warned when she looked away, out of the window, down at the floor. Anything other than look him straight in the eye. 'He didn't come with you, did he?'

'No.'

It was just a whisper, the barest thread of sound, and she

drew invisible patterns on the floor with the toe of one bare foot, watching the process with an intensity that was totally unconvincing.

'No, he's not here. In fact he won't be coming at all. Not ever.'

'Not even when the baby…?'

'No.'

She shook her head again, her expression that of a forlorn child.

'He won't come for me, or for the baby. He doesn't want either of us. He never did. Not really. He was just having a bit of fun—playing around. As a matter of fact…'

She drew in another of those deep breaths that he had come to realise always preceded another of the announcements that were so shockingly disturbing to his emotional equilibrium.

'He's married.'

'Married? Oh, Meggie, Meggie, you little *fool*!'

'I didn't know!'

Indignation rang sharp in her voice.

'Do you think I'd even have gone out with—for one night alone if I'd known! If I'd so much as suspected? I'm not that much of an idiot!'

'No?' Once more those black eyebrows rose, cynically questioning her assertion. 'It seems to me…'

'Oh, I know how it seems to you—to the great, the all-knowing—the supremely infallible Cesare Santorino!'

Bitterness darkened Megan's tone as she swung away to stare moodily into the empty fireplace.

'We all know that you would never, ever make a mistake like that!'

'Oh, wouldn't I?' Cesare muttered bleakly, half to himself.

He made a mistake all right, coming here tonight, like

this! Made a complete and total fool of himself! He'd thought of nothing else but this moment. Of the time when, freed from his promise to Megan's father, he could declare the way he felt about her, the torch he'd been carrying for her for years as he'd watched her develop from a child into an adolescent and then into a beautiful young woman.

But he'd deceived himself totally into thinking that she felt something of the same. That she would wait for him, as he had determined to wait for her. She hadn't waited! Hadn't even thought about him! Instead she'd jumped straight into bed with someone else—a married man at that!

And how was he to know that this Gary had been the first?

The blazing rage that had been burning inside him stilled suddenly, the red-hot flames turning blue and icy. And cold fury was even harder to deal with than heated anger. Bitterness was cold—and jealousy—and hatred. And he hated even to think of Megan—his lovely, sweet *innocent* Megan in bed with someone else—giving herself to someone else!

He had never felt such an icy burn in his heart before. It stung like acid, seeming to eat away at his soul, leaving it broken and ruined, with great dark holes where his emotions should be.

'And when was that?' Megan's voice broke into the blackness of his thoughts, jarring him out of the brooding darkness and into the present again, making him unwillingly aware of the way that she had turned back from the fire and was now staring at him in puzzled confusion.

'What?' he responded, struggling to get himself back under control. 'What did you say?'

'I wanted to know just when you made this great mistake you're talking about,' Megan told him. 'What was this terrible thing you did and when?'

Idiota! Cesare cursed himself inwardly. You fool! You

damn, damn fool! Now he'd alerted her attention, piquing her curiosity and centring it on him. And just when he was least capable of handling her questions. When he had only just realised how badly he'd misjudged everything and was incapable of explaining anything to her—if in fact he'd wanted to do any explaining!

On the contrary, he was determined that she should never find out how he had felt. He had come here tonight with the determination to tell Megan just that. To declare the instant attraction to her that had never faded over the years. To say that deep inside he actually believed he loved her and that he wanted her to spend the rest of her life with him.

But her rash words, her blunt declaration, had damaged those dreams beyond repair. He doubted if he would ever admit to them. He would never tell her how he felt—how he *had* felt, because he didn't feel that way any more.

If the truth was told, he had no idea how he felt at all.

'Cesare…' Megan persisted, soft, but insistent.

'Oh, it was nothing!' he bluffed, veiling his eyes behind long black lashes in order to hide the truth from her. 'Like you, I fell in love with the wrong person.'

'And when was that?'

'Years ago. I was little more than a child. Same age as you if you must know.'

It was like a slap in the face, Megan reflected miserably. A cool-voiced reminder that he thought of her as little more than an awkward, troublesome adolescent. Nothing had changed then since his brutal dismissal of her just over six months before.

'Except that, unlike me, you didn't end up with—unfortunate consequences!' she tossed back, hiding pain behind sarcasm.

Don't you believe it! Hastily Cesare bit the words back.

Unfortunate consequences! He had given his heart into the keeping of a child. Put his life on hold until she was old enough to be his—and now she had turned out to be someone else entirely.

'I got over it,' he returned, lacing the words with acid. 'You do. What is it you say—time heals all wounds.'

'Except that in my case, time can only make things worse.' Unthinkingly Megan touched a hand to her lower body, bringing Cesare's dark-eyed gaze to the spot.

'Are you sure?'

'As sure as I can be.'

'Have you seen a doctor?'

'Cesare, I don't need to see a doctor. I know what's happening to me! I haven't had a period for the past two months and I was always regular as clockwork—same time same day. I've been feeling sick in the mornings—and I did one of those horrible tests from the chemists. It came up positive.'

'I understand that those things aren't always accurate.'

'Stop clutching at straws, Cesare! I'm pregnant. There's no two ways about it!'

'So what are you going to do about it?'

'I don't know,' Megan admitted honestly.

'You're not thinking of an abortion?'

If he hadn't been such a great businessman, then Cesare could have had a great career as an interrogator, Megan found herself thinking. He fired the questions at her, cold and hard and fierce, like rounds of bullets from a machine-gun, hardly giving her time to think. She had had enough of his stony-faced disapproval, that cold-eyed, critical glare.

'No, I'm not thinking of an abortion! I couldn't and I wouldn't! Not that it's any business of yours!'

'I was only trying to help!'

'By suggesting that I got rid of my baby? I can do without that sort of *help*!'

'Megan, that isn't what I meant!'

'Isn't it? Sounded like it to me! Well, can I remind you, Signor Santorino, that this is *my* baby! And as such it has nothing whatsoever to do with you!'

'Which, *Signorina* Ellis,' Cesare returned viciously. 'Is exactly the way I want it.'

'Fine!' Megan tossed her head as she spoke, her russet hair flying, her chin coming up in defiance. 'I'm glad we understand each other!'

'Oh, we do!' Cesare returned darkly. 'Believe me, I understand perfectly! And as I prefer not to stay around when it is made so patently clear that my company is not welcome, I'll say goodnight.'

'At last! I thought you'd never leave!'

She saw his dark head go back sharply at the spite in her tone and knew with a deep, tearing sense of regret that she had succeeded far better than she had ever anticipated in making him think she couldn't stand the sight of him. The real fact was that nothing could be further from the truth.

Or did she mean that nothing could be *closer* to the truth?

She didn't know. Couldn't decide whether she couldn't wait to see the back of him, and would frankly be delighted if she never saw or heard from Cesare Santorino again in all her life. Or if the terrible suspicion that her heart would break if he left now and never came back was in fact the true one and the determined anger only a camouflage shield, thrown up to protect herself from the truth.

'I'll see you around.'

She was so choked up that she could only nod in response to his curt goodbye. She knew that her silence made her look even colder and more distant than ever but it was all that she could manage. A cold, cruel hand was clutching at her throat, cutting off all her ability to speak and she knew that if she so much as opened her mouth she would burst into tears or find some other way of making a total fool of herself.

So she watched in silence as he spun on his heel and walked away from her. She had always known that the library was a big room, a long room, but never before had the walk from the bay window where she stood to the door seemed so protracted, so endless.

And Cesare seemed to be deliberately taking his time about it. Or was that her deceiving herself? Because he never paused; never hesitated or looked back. He just kept putting one foot in front of another in his determined march away from her.

Still silent, she watched him cross the polished wooden floor, then the thick dark red and cream rug, then the floor again. She almost spoke then but caught back the words, clamping her lips tight on them. She let him get to the door, watched those strong fingers close around the handle, turn it…

'Cesare!'

His name burst from her, impossible to hold back.

'Cesare, *please*!'

He had thought she was going to let him go. He told himself it was what he wanted. That he was leaving, right now, for good! He was never, ever coming back. The crazy dreams of love and marriage and forever that had been in his thoughts when he had arrived at the house had crumbled into dust. He could almost imagine he was trampling them into the ground as he walked.

He was leaving. He didn't know where he was going, but he knew it would be via the nearest bar. *Dio*, but he could do with a drink!

And then she spoke. Just his name, on a whisper so quiet and soft that at first he wasn't at all sure he had heard anything. And his march towards the door was so determined, so unstoppable that he barely hesitated. He even grasped the handle of the door and turned it.

'Cesare, *please*!'

It stopped him dead in his tracks, still with his hand on the door.

'Please don't go!'

How could he resist the appealing in that voice; the slight, shaken tremble on the first word that had clearly escaped her in spite of her determination not to let it. For a couple of seconds, feeling fought a nasty little battle with rational thought—thought reminding him of how he had felt a moment earlier, the kicked-in-the-teeth sensation that had followed her announcement. He tried hard to revive some of the fury, the disgust, the burning jealousy. And failed.

And then, as he had known it must inevitably do, emotion won. There was no way he could resist that appeal to his sympathy. And so, letting his hand drop again, he turned back to face her.

'What do you want, Megan?'

She was still standing exactly where he had left her, her slender body stiffly upright, fine-boned arms hanging loose at her sides. She was so pale—ashen—that her eyes seemed unnaturally dark above her bloodless cheeks, and the skin looked as if it was stretched taut over the high, slanting cheekbones.

The way that all the life seemed to have been drained out of her was shocking. She looked like a washed-out, faded, version of her real self. The only real trace of colour in her face was her mouth. Clearly those white teeth had been worrying at her lower lip, bringing the blood rushing to the surface, so that it glowed, shockingly bright and red.

With a deep inward sigh, Cesare accepted that he would never, ever, be able to leave while she looked like this.

'Tell me what you want and I'll do it.'

Tell me what you want and I'll do it. Cesare's mouth spoke the words, Megan registered, but his eyes were cold, distant, dead, no trace of emotion in them. He had clearly made himself speak because he had no other option, but there was no kindness, no caring in the words.

'Please don't leave...'

It was all she could manage and she heard his harshly indrawn sigh of impatience at her inanity.

'I'm not leaving, Megan. Not if you want me here. Just tell me what you want me to do.'

'I don't know what to do!'

It was the cry of a frightened child, and the hand that she held out towards him shook with the force of the feelings she was struggling to control.

If he touched that hand he was lost. He could still feel the softness of her skin under his fingertips. If he licked his lips he would still taste her on his tongue. The scent of her body was in his nostrils, a potent mixture of her personal perfume and the warmth of vanilla and lily that she wore on every pulse point.

Just to think of the way it had felt to hold her, to kiss her, made his libido give him a sharp, painful kick. Without the fury of frustration to distract him and push it from his thoughts, the nag of desire was like a bruise in his mind, clamouring urgently for attention. But he couldn't give in to it. There was no way he could give it free rein, indulge the need he felt.

Bitterly he cursed the fool who had appeared on the doorstep earlier that evening. He had been so sure, so full of himself, so damn confident. He had thought that all he had to do was to walk in and Megan would be his for the taking.

Well, he'd been pretty efficiently disillusioned on that score!

But still, when she looked at him like this, there was no way he could just walk out and leave her. It would be like abandoning some baby fawn in a forest prowled by ravenous wolves.

'You need to be practical. I take it you want to keep this baby?'

'You take it right!' Megan replied with a slight return of something like her old spirit. 'I'm not—'

'And I'm not asking you to,' Cesare put in hastily, seeing the threat of tears in the suspicious brightness of her eyes. 'It was just one of your possible options. And you're sure that the father won't help?'

'Gary?'

Her faint shudder was expressive of just how she felt on that matter.

'He made his opinion perfectly plain. I was just a passing fling—someone he amused himself with while he was here in England. He was a visiting lecturer at the university, over here from America. He neglected to tell anyone that he had a wife and two children back in the States. He certainly wasn't in the market for a third little Gary Rowell!'

'He sounds a real charmer!'

'That was the trouble—he was—charming I mean. He—'

'I don't want to hear any more about him!'

Already the plague twist of jealousy was making his pulse throb at his temple, threatening his precarious hold on his mood. Clamping down on the dangerous thoughts, refusing to let them take root, he moved forward to take her by the hand and draw her away from the window.

'Come and sit down. We can talk better if you're more comfortable. And you look dead on your feet.'

'I am tired,' Megan admitted. 'I haven't been sleeping very well.'

'I can imagine.'

He was heading towards the burgundy settee when the awareness of her hesitation, a reluctance in her step made him realise. She wasn't exactly pulling back but still it was plain enough, without a word having to be said, that the site of their recent near lovemaking wasn't the most tactful of places to choose to discuss the delicate topics they needed to cover. So he carefully changed direction, subtly, he hoped, and settled her in a large, comfortable armchair, on the far side of the fireplace.

Oh, damnation. This was worse, if anything. From where they sat, the settee seemed to loom, unnaturally large and solid, the crushed and disordered cushions speaking disturbingly eloquently of the passion that had flared so briefly yet so hotly between them such a short time before.

Megan shot the inoffensive piece of furniture one swift, slanting look of loathing, the sort of look one might direct at a deadly snake that had appeared, before she subsided into the chair and hastily averted her eyes.

Well, that had put him well and truly in his place, Cesare reflected bitterly. If his lovemaking was so repugnant to her then he was unlikely to even think of attempting anything similar in the future.

Which meant giving up once and for all on the dream he had held for so long. As soon as the idea had formed inside his head, he knew he couldn't accept defeat so easily. But there seemed no other possible way forward.

Unless…

Suddenly another idea came to him. A way that, maybe after all, he could have what he had always wanted. It

wouldn't be the perfect accomplishment of that dream perhaps, not the way he had thought it might be one day. But
experience had taught him that very few things were actually ever perfect and that sometimes you just had to settle
for second best or nothing at all.

'So have you told your father?'

Megan was shocked just at the thought of it. She shook
her head vehemently, unable even to think of the prospect
without horror.

'I couldn't! He has enough on his plate right now.'

'And you are not exactly going through the easiest
months of your life.'

'But Dad is worried sick already. And if what you said
is true, then he's right to be so. I can't possibly add to that.
He's fighting for his life—well, the only life he's ever really known. And he hasn't been well lately. He has high
blood pressure, heart problems—can you think what it
would do to him if I added this to the burdens he's already
dealing with?'

'So what are you going to do? Can you support yourself?'

'I don't know. I'll have to try. I'm sure I could find
something. Though a History of Art degree isn't exactly
the most practical subject to offer to a prospective employer.'

'There is an alternative.'

'There is?'

Megan's expression brightened considerably, a new light
coming into the shadowed depths of her eyes.

Cesare nodded slowly, his expression disturbingly sombre. Whatever he was about to suggest, Megan was suddenly not at all sure she was going to like it.

'There's marriage.'

Her glance was a bitter reproach.

'But I told you before that Gary…'

'Not to that rat!'

An arrogant flick of one hand dismissed the other man as not even worth the effort of remembering his name.

'Then who? I don't exactly see a long line of suitors queuing up to ask for the honour of my hand in marriage. Nor are they likely to now!'

'You're missing the obvious.'

'I am?'

Bewildered, she looked into his dark, stunning face, hunting for an answer.

'I don't—who?'

'There's me. You could marry me.'

CHAPTER FOUR

'Oн!'

It was all she could manage. Shock, disbelief and pain at a very sick joke—because it had to be a joke!—combined to deprive her of any capability of speech and she cold stared at him in bitter distress, unable to believe that he could be so cruel. The brilliant ebony eyes looked back at her steadily, unwavering, totally serious. Shockingly so.

Her heart jolted, clenched in something close to panic. He couldn't mean it! But his expression said that he did.

'You're joking!'

'*Al contrario*, I do not think I have been more serious in my life. It would solve both our problems at a stroke.'

'Both?'

She wished he wouldn't tower over her like that. She was having to crane her neck to look up at him and he seemed so powerful, so *big*, so intensely physical that it was scrambling her brain simply being in the same room as him. And she had to think. Had to try and consider what he had said with some sort of rationality. Because no matter how wild, how crazy, how *impossible* it seemed, she had to accept that Cesare was in deadly earnest about this.

'What sort of problem do you have that marriage to me will help solve?'

'My family.'

As if he had known her thoughts earlier, he now came closer, perching himself elegantly on the arm of the chair and looking down into her upturned face.

And immediately, perversely, Megan wished he was any-

52

where but there. Every sense seemed to be on red-alert, awakening and responding to his closeness—and he was *too* close. Close enough to see the dark shadow on his jaw line where he needed a shave, to scent the tang of his cologne, the intensely personal fragrance of his skin. Her heartbeat was rough and uneven, making it difficult to breathe naturally.

She wanted to look away, but found she couldn't. That deep, coffee-coloured gaze held hers so that she couldn't look anywhere but into the depths of his eyes. She saw how the darkness of his iris had expanded, widening until there was nothing but the faintest rim of brown at its edges, and she didn't dare to ask herself why that might be.

'What about your family?' she managed. 'Why should they be involved in this?'

'They want me to marry and have a family. Children to inherit the company, to take charge of it in the future. Everyone thought that Gio would have more children, but obviously, since Lucia died, that's not going to be so now.'

Megan nodded sombrely, recognising and understanding the shadows that suddenly clouded his eyes. His older half-brother, Gio, had been deeply in love, happily married, but then one day his beautiful wife Lucia had died unexpectedly. A brain haemorrhage, the doctors had said, something that could not be predicted, nor could anything have been done to help her.

'But wouldn't you want a proper marriage?'

'We could have a proper marriage. We've always got on well enough, haven't we? And what happened just now…'

His dark eyes slid to the settee, rested for a moment on the rumpled cushions that still had not been restored to order. Watching him, seeing the emotionless expression on his face, the way his lids hooded his eyes, hiding what was in them, Megan felt hot colour rise in her face and she bit down hard on her lower lip to hold back the sound of discomfort that almost escaped her. She needed no reminder to tell her that how she had behaved in those mad, erotically charged moments, had been way out of character. She had never ever responded to anyone in that way before, not even, she admitted, to Gary, whom she thought she had loved.

'Surely that told you that we had one thing going for us? And at New Year...'

'At New Year I'd had one glass too many of champagne,' Megan put in hastily, not wanting any more reminders of the foolish ways she had behaved. 'I was lonely and unsure of myself and—well you were around.'

'So all those protestations of undying love weren't meant?'

'No more than your proposal just now—if it was a proposal.'

'Yes, it was a proposal, and believe me, unlike you, I meant every single word of it. So what's your answer?'

'What else do you think it can be but no? No, I won't marry you—as you always knew I wouldn't.'

If she hadn't known better, she would have sworn that just for a moment a flicker of something that could almost have been disappointment flashed through his eyes. But he couldn't have felt any such emotion—at least no more than he might have experienced if some business deal he had been intent on achieving had failed, when he had been sure of a very different result.

'You're saying no?'

It brought her an absurd sense of delight and satisfaction to know that she had shocked him. Did he really think her such a naïve fool that she would fall into his arms simply because he offered? Or was he so supremely arrogant that he just couldn't imagine *any* woman turning him down?

'Yes, I'm saying no!' Deliberately she adopted a tone of excessive politeness, every syllable stiff with precise English formality. 'Thank you for your kind offer of marriage, Signor Santorino, but I'm afraid I shall have to de— to decline the—the honour...'

Somehow in the face of his unmoving, unblinking, cold-eyed scrutiny, the words seemed to get tangled up on her tongue so that she had to struggle to get them out.

'The honour of becoming your wife. It's just not for me.'

Well, that put him in his place, Cesare reflected ruefully. And he was quite unprepared for the way it made him feel. It was ridiculous—unbelievable—that he found himself floundering, not knowing what to say. Give him a business meeting, or a contract discussion any day. He could negotiate other directors, other CEOs, under the table before breakfast and come back for more. But this one small, slight slip of a girl had him tied up in knots, unsure of which tack to try next.

But he damn well wasn't giving in. Not until he was sure he had no other argument to offer, no other enticement to persuade her to give in. And he *was* going to get her to surrender, he vowed. He wasn't leaving here until she agreed to become his wife. It was either that or walk away from her for ever. And that was something he was just not prepared to countenance.

He knew that in the business world there was a saying. 'Sooner tangle with a hungry lion than with a determined Santorino.' Well, tonight Megan Ellis was going to wish she'd come up against the starving man-eater instead of him.

'You must have known I couldn't accept.'

'I knew no such thing.'

With an impatient movement, Cesare pushed himself up from the chair arm and strode to the huge, empty fireplace, staring broodily down at it for a long moment. Then he swung round to face her again.

'So would you mind telling me just what you're going to do instead?'

'Do?'

Megan's eyes clouded with confusion and the momentary mask of confidence she had assumed wavered sharply, threatening to dissolve and reveal the true depths of her insecurity.

'I—I'll manage. Somehow. There'll be something…'

'Give me an example.'

Cesare was back in attacking mode.

'Two minutes ago, you were adrift on a black sea of fear. "I don't know what to do".' He echoed her own cry of panic with disturbing accuracy. 'Now suddenly you're Miss Independence personified. I'm forced to wonder what brought about the change. Is the idea of marriage to me so terribly repugnant?'

'Of course not!'

She tried for laughter, missed it by a mile. Because the truth was that amusement was so very far from the way she was feeling. If only he knew that for years of her life, almost all the time she had been growing up, in fact, marriage to Cesare Santorino had been her one great dream. The fantasy that he might one day ask her to be his wife had been something she had hugged to herself in secret, only letting it out to look at in the late, dark hours and the privacy of her bedroom, just before she fell asleep.

'I told you I was honoured…'

The blackly sceptical look he turned on her made the words shrivel on her tongue.

'Could you really take on another man's child?'

'It wouldn't be another man's child. You gave Rowell the chance to make it his; he didn't take it. He's not fit to be the baby's father. Your child would be born inside our marriage. It would only ever know me as its father. I would take care of the baby as I would take care of you.'

'I can take care of myself!'

'Oh, sure!'

'Other people manage!'

'Other people have to,' Cesare stated flatly. 'They have no alternative. I'm offering you a choice. You won't have to *manage*. You'll be able to take care of your child properly, give it everything it needs.'

He was getting through to her. She was tempted at least. He could see that from the faint wavering of that moss-green gaze, a flicker of uncertainty deep in her eyes. And there was one more argument he could use to persuade her.

'If you like, I'll even throw in a rescue package for your father as part of the deal.'

'You make it sound like a business deal!'

Cesare's shrug of supreme indifference dismissed her protest as totally irrelevant.

'But like all the best business contracts, it's one in which we both get what we want.'

Taking several swift, long strides towards her, he bent his head and looked deep into her eyes.

'What's wrong, Meggie?' he questioned softly. 'Was my proposal too matter-of-fact for you? Not romantic enough? Would you have preferred it if I'd gone down on one knee...'

To her horror he suited action to the words, sinking gracefully down onto one knee so that his dark, handsome face was almost on a level with hers as she sat in the chair. Reaching for her hand, he folded his own, long, powerful fingers around it and clasped it firmly.

'Megan...' he began, his voice deep and resonant, his

eyes burning into hers. 'Would you do me the very great honour of becoming my wife?'

'Oh, stop it!'

Shocked and distressed, Megan made a sharp movement of her hand, trying to snatch it away from his. But the hard fingers closed around hers restrained her without any effort.

'Please be serious!'

'I am serious. I doubt if I've ever been more serious in my life.'

It was only when the carved contours of his face began to blur in front of her that Megan became bitterly aware of the tears that were threatening, collecting at the back of her eyes and pushing to slide out, trickle revealingly down her cheeks.

Blinking hard, she struggled to force them back. She wasn't prepared to let Cesare see them; was too afraid of what they betrayed—even to herself.

It was as if she had slipped back in time. Back to a point where Cesare Santorino had been the only man in the world for her. When he had filled her waking thoughts by day, her dreams at night. And one of those recurring dreams had been of a moment just like this one, when the tall, handsome and charismatic Italian was on his knees before her, begging her to be his bride.

And now he was doing just that—but he was only proposing because he could think of no other alternative that solved both their problems, and his proposition had been made like a business pitch, no emotion involved at all. And it was the way that lack of emotion hurt, biting deep into her soul, that warned her of the real danger she was in.

'Cesare, you must know that I can't marry you!'

'I know that you can't do anything else. Certainly not anything that will give you the freedom and the money to be a full-time mother to your child, and help your father out of his problems all in one go. You must know that Tom won't be able to support you—he'll be hard pushed to support himself if his business goes to the wall.'

Megan felt as if she was being sucked inexorably and irresistibly into the future that Cesare had planned for her, no matter how hard she kicked and screamed, trying desperately to drag herself away from the seductive appeal of all he offered.

'I wouldn't want my father to support me. It would be like staying as a child all my life instead of becoming an adult.'

'But in a marriage with me, we would be equal partners. And what could be more grown-up than being a wife and a mother?'

He had an answer for everything, it seemed, and she was fast running out of questions and objections.

'Cesare, will you please get up off your knees!' she begged but he shook his proud head in adamant rejection of her plea.

'Not until you give me your answer.'

'I've given it to you!'

Even in her own ears, the slight break between the first and second words, a quiver at the end of the sentence robbed the declaration of any real strength and conviction.

'Not the answer I want. See sense, Megan!'

Sense didn't come into it. There was a bitter irony in being handed her adolescent dream on a plate but in a way that threatened to deprive her of any happiness in it. What she had always dreamed of was having Cesare fall madly in love with her. The prospect of that happening seemed as far away as ever.

But perhaps if they were together, in close proximity, for some time? And what could be closer than to live as man and wife, sharing the same life, the same home—a cold hand twisted in her stomach making her shiver faintly—the same *bed*.

And, even as she acknowledged it, she knew that the shiver that ran through her was not one of fear, but on the contrary it had been a disturbing sense of excitement, a thrill of anticipation at just the thought of consummating what they had started here tonight.

'*Dannazione*, Megan, you must know we could make this work! We've always got on well together—we like each other, which is more than even some married couples can say! And you have to admit that the physical fire that sparked between us tonight can only mean that at least that side of things is taken care of.'

'There's more to a marriage than sex.'

Oh, why—*why* was she still fighting him? Why was she fighting *herself*? Wasn't the truth the fact that it would be so much easier, so much simpler, just to give in and agree? And deep down, wasn't this what she had always wanted all along?

And now, when she was totally unprepared for it, when the last thing she wanted to do was remember it, an image came into her mind of the first time she had met Gary Rowell. Tall and darkly handsome, the visiting lecturer had reminded her instantly of Cesare. They could have been brothers, apart from the fact that the American's eyes were blue where Cesare's were the deepest, darkest brown she had ever seen. And, still smarting from Cesare's heartless rejection of her, the scornful way he had dismissed her declarations of love at the New Year party, she had fallen into the other man's arms like a very ripe plum indeed. A naïve and gullible plum that had believed every lying word of love that had fallen from his lips, swallowing his pro-testations of devotion and promises of happily ever after because they were what she most needed to hear.

'I know there's more to a marriage than sex, but, *diavolo*, Megan, it's a good place to start. It gives us something to build on.'

Maybe she was grasping at straws, but 'something to build on' seemed to imply rather more than just a business deal. Was she being all sorts of a fool in letting herself hope that Cesare's words implied a chance of a real life together, a future, a real marriage?

'Megan…'

Her name was a low, bad-tempered growl as Cesare shifted slightly, adjusting his position on the rug before her.

'Are you ever going to give me an answer, because if not I swear to God that I'm going to get up off this damnably uncomfortable floor and walk right out of here. And I warn you that if I do, I'll go for good. I'll walk out and never come back, and you can beg and plead for help all you like, but I won't listen. You can kiss goodbye to my promise to bail out both you and your father, because I won't be putting that offer on the table ever again.'

He meant it too; she could have no doubt about that. And the thought of seeing him walk away from her, walking out of her life, panicked her into an unthinking response.

'Will you really help my father out?'

'I could hardly leave my father-in-law as a bankrupt. I'll pay each and every debt of his just as soon as our marriage certificate is signed. But only then. And you have to give me an answer now. No asking for time to think, or a chance to sleep on it. It's a once in a lifetime offer. Now or never. Don't hope to get back to me tomorrow because if you do…'

'I won't need to! I can give you your answer now.'

The words were out before she had time to think if they were wise, or even if she could cope with the sort of future

they represented. She only knew that she couldn't say anything else. She couldn't let him go. She had no idea what
the future might hold with him, but a future *without* Cesare
in it was something she couldn't bear to even begin to
imagine.

'So...' Cesare prompted with renewed impatience when,
having made her impetuous declaration she froze, unable
to go any further. 'What is this answer?'

The look Megan turned on him was one filled with reproach and a touch of bitterness at the way he had trapped
her. Even while admitting that he was right, that she got
what she wanted, she wished that she could have had some
sort of choice in the matter.

'You know what it is, Cesare! You know there's only
one answer I can give you! After all, you've pushed me
into a corner with my back well and truly up against the
wall.'

'So it's yes.'

His tone held no trace of doubt, instead it was full of a
dark, ruthless satisfaction and at last he stood up, flexing
his shoulders and brushing down the legs of his impeccably
tailored trousers.

'*Buono*! I will put things in motion. We will need a special licence, and then...'

'Put things in...!'

Megan couldn't believe the swiftness of the transfor-
mation. One moment, her suitor had been down on one
knee, waiting for an answer to his proposal; the next he
was back in killer businessman mode once again, planning,
organising, making lists, taking her life right out of her
hands and arranging it to suit himself without so much as
a by your leave.

'Don't you think—'

The impatient glare Cesare turned in her direction silenced her at once.

'Megan, we have no time to waste. You are *incinta*. If we are to be married before you start to show then we must move quickly. A special licence is the only way.'

'But does it matter what people think? I mean you and I...'

Once more he quelled her with a slanting, dark-eyed look.

'It matters to me! I do not want anyone knowing the truth about this marriage. I don't want any suspicion that it is not a love match—a genuine whirlwind romance—entering anyone's thoughts. And I'm sure you'll feel that way too.'

'Well, it certainly would be one in the eye for Gary to think that I could forget about him so soon, and fall for someone else almost straight away.'

He didn't like her words; the dark scowl on his face told her that, but she was past caring. His businesslike manner hurt. It hurt badly. But what had she expected? Some expression of deep gratitude for the fact that she had accepted his proposal? Some declaration of undying love? A promise to make her happy for the rest of her life?

She would be all sorts of a dreamer and a fool if she had wished for any such thing. What Cesare had proposed was a marriage of convenience, nothing more, nothing less; and she couldn't ask for anything else. But how many women would have just accepted a proposal of marriage and had that followed by a strictly businesslike discussion of all they needed to arrange? Surely she could have expected *something*? Some touch of affection. A kiss—even a smile?

'What is it?' Cesare's tone was sharp, his frown growing deeper. 'You look as if someone had just pronounced your death sentence in a court of law.'

Perhaps someone had, Megan couldn't help thinking. Perhaps by agreeing to Cesare's coldly rational and unemotional proposal, *she* was the one who had signed the death warrant of her own hopes and dreams of a happily ever after and a lifetime of love.

'I was just wondering what you'd get out of this arrangement.'

'I told you—I'll get just what I want.'

'And that is?'

'A wife—a child.'

'A child that's not yours.'

His shrug was one of total indifference.

'Who'd know? Who'd care? It'd get my parents off my back—and we could have others. I always wanted a large family.'

'And that would be enough—No?' she managed on a rather strangled gasp as once more he shook his head.

'Oh, no, *mia cara*, there is no way that could ever be enough. If that was all that I had ever wanted, I could have asked a dozen women—more—to marry me over the years, but I did not.'

The dark eyes locked with hers, holding her gaze with the force of a mesmerist so that it was impossible to look away; to look anywhere but into their depths.

When had he come so close? she asked herself, her heart giving a nervous little flutter against the side of her ribcage. She hadn't noticed him move and yet it seemed that suddenly his body was mere inches away. She could almost feel the imprint of its strength, the hardness of bone and muscle, the heat of skin searing into her at breasts and hips and thighs, all that was most feminine in her leaping in a wild, instinctive response that was as old and as primitive as time.

'Why…'

Her throat was painfully dry and she had to swallow convulsively to ease it. But even then, when she tried to speak again, her voice still croaked embarrassingly, coming and going in the most peculiar way.

'Why didn't you ask them?' she managed, knowing that it was what he wanted her to say.

Cesare's smile was slow, almost benign, but there was something in his eyes that stopped it from being the tender response it appeared. There was a hint of danger in that look; the threat of something she neither knew nor understood. But as he drew her to her feet, she couldn't pull away. Couldn't move or do anything to distract him or turn aside what she knew was coming.

'They didn't offer me what I wanted,' he said with a deliberate softness.

Automatically Megan lowered her voice to match his.

'And that was…?' she whispered and watched his smile grow into a wicked, demonic grin.

'This…'

She had barely time to catch her breath before his mouth came down on hers, but it was with an unexpected gentleness that seemed to draw out her soul, take it away from her and hold it captive. And in that moment she knew that she was lost. Knew that no matter how hard she tried to convince herself, no matter what stories she made up to explain it, there was no way in the world that she was *over* Cesare Santorino.

She hadn't been over him at New Year, when he had scorned her love, refusing her urgently offered kisses, shrugging off her clinging hands, and telling her to find a boy her own age to play with. And she hadn't been over him when she had fallen into Gary's arms, lost and alone and desperate on the rebound from that rejection. Looking for love anywhere, with anyone, and thinking she had found it with quite the wrong man entirely.

And so she couldn't hold back now, but melted against him, letting him plunder her mouth, gentleness changing to demand in the space of a heartbeat. From there demand became heated passion, a passion that she met and welcomed, her mouth opening under his to return the kiss with all the burning urgency that her yearning emotions, the emptiness in her soul clamoured for. Just for a second she felt Cesare's momentary check, the tiny hesitation that told her how her reaction was unexpected, but then he too was kissing her back with that same need, that same hunger, that couldn't be controlled.

And at last his arms closed round her, urgent hands moving over her body, stroking, caressing, teasing, tantalising. Unerringly his knowing fingers found tiny pleasure spots that made her sigh or move convulsively against him. When the strength of those hands slid under the white cotton of her T-shirt and pushed their way up to close over the curves of her breasts which had been aching for just such a touch, she moaned aloud against his tormenting mouth. Her own hands went up, closing over the hard strength of his shoulders, clinging on for support for fear her legs might actually give way and she would fall in a weak, swooning heap at his feet.

But then, just when she thought she could take no more. When she thought she must faint, or cry, or give in to the feelings that were boiling up inside her, and actually put her need for him into words. Just when she had opened her mouth to tell him of her need, of the longing she felt, to beg him to take her, to make love to her right here and now, to make her his, he lifted his proud head and looked long and hard into her clouded eyes.

'*That* is what I wanted,' he said, and she felt a sort of

primal satisfaction at hearing the way that his voice had a rough and ragged edge to it, telling her that for all his outward composure, inwardly he was as deeply affected as she had been.

'That is how I always wanted things to be,' he went on. 'How I always knew they could be. That's why I never asked anyone else—never even thought of asking them. I knew that's how it would be with you and me, and I knew you'd be worth waiting for. You asked what I would get out of this arrangement—this marriage. The answer is that I get you. And I *want* you. I want you more than life itself. I always have and I always will.'

CHAPTER FIVE

'I NOW pronounce you husband and wife.'

Behind them, the organ music swelled up into the rafters of the church. The collection of family and friends—as many as could be collected together in the very short space of time that there had been between the announcement of the impending wedding and the actual event—turned to each other and smiled at the sound of the familiar words. And Cesare could almost hear the collected sigh of satisfaction that the moment for which they had been waiting had finally arrived.

But it was the woman beside him who held his attention.

Megan Ellis, now Megan Santorino, stood at his side, tall, slender and elegant in the simple sleeveless ivory silk dress, her bright hair caught up at the sides and decorated with a couple of soft cream rosebuds that were just beginning to unfurl in the heat and release their perfume into the air.

From this moment on, the scent of roses would always mean his wedding day, the beginning of his married life. But what future was there in store for that marriage? He had rushed into it impetuously, making up his mind in a second, in a way that none of his friends or business associates would recognise.

Cesare Santorino *never* rushed into anything. His reputation was that he took his time, collected all the facts, learned everything there was to learn about the contract or the situation before he committed himself to anything. Only

68

when he was certain that everything was exactly the way he wanted it, did he sign any document.

And yet now here he was, married to Megan on what was little more than an impulse, signing away his life without knowing the full facts about the situation.

'You may kiss your bride.'

His bride.

Yes, she was his in the eyes of the law, the church, or of the congregation here present, but was she truly *his*? Did she think of herself as his wife or was he nothing more than the man who'd stepped in to get her out of a tight spot? A husband of convenience. A husband in name only.

Someone who could never, ever, be the husband of her heart.

Had he just made the very worst mistake of his life?

But everyone was watching him, waiting for him to make his move and kiss his brand-new wife. The clergyman was waiting too.

And Megan.

Megan was looking up at him, eyes dark with something he couldn't even begin to interpret. But as she saw his gaze turn to her she managed a smile. A soft, strangely tentative smile. One that started out brave and encouraging, a smile of sharing, linking them like a couple of co-conspirators united together against the world.

But as he watched the smile lost its façade of confidence. It wavered, weakened, frayed at the edges and suddenly faded altogether, leaving Megan's face looking pale and wan, disturbingly young and lost.

'Meggie...'

In a sudden rush of tenderness, he reached for her, enfolded her in his arms, drew her close. One hand came under her chin, lifted her face to his, green eyes locking with deep, dark brown.

'*Buon giorno*, Signora Santorino,' he murmured, for her ears only. '*Buon giorno, mia moglie.*'

And bending his head he took her mouth in their first kiss as husband and wife.

And even here, in this public place, with their audience of family and friends just a few feet away from them, her response was everything he wanted. Her mouth softened under his, opening to even the gentlest pressure. Her body swayed towards his like a compass point drawn irresistibly to the north, and she closed her eyes slowly, giving herself up to the caress in a way that made his lower body tighten in an immediate and powerfully primitive reaction that was definitely out of place within the confines of a church.

She was his, he told himself with grim satisfaction, pushing away all the doubts and uncertainties of moments before, and, damn it, he would make sure she stayed that way. She was his to have and to hold and he'd *hold* her all right. He'd hold her tight and never let her go. And perhaps one day, when the pain of loving Gary, and the other man's— the rat's—betrayal had eased, maybe then she'd come to care for him.

Diavolo! He swore in the privacy of his thoughts, he'd make bloody sure she did! And perhaps, after all, from this most imperfect of beginnings, they could build something worth having, something worth keeping.

'*Buon giorno*, Signora Santorino.' The words echoed inside Megan's head. '*Buon giorno, mia moglie.*'

Was it possible? Was she really and truly no longer simply Megan Ellis, but Megan *Santorino*—Cesare's wife?

Just the thought of it made her heart turn over, her pulse race. The thought of what she'd done, and its implications for the future were simply terrifying. She and Cesare were married, committed for life, and she had no idea what he truly felt about the situation.

In the moment that the celebrant had murmured the traditional encouragement to 'kiss the bride' she had turned to face this new husband of hers, trying to smile through her nervousness, to communicate something of the way she felt, to let him know that they were a couple now, facing the future and what it might bring together.

But the look he had turned on her had been so blank, so distant, the ebony depths of his eyes withdrawn and impenetrable, so that she had known she hadn't touched him. Hadn't reached through to his mind, let alone his heart, which remained as closed and locked from her as ever. Her feelings, her *love*, were clearly not what he wanted from her, nor, she doubted, would they ever be.

But her passion, her sexuality, her body—that was another matter entirely. *That* he had made only too plain was what he wanted, and he emphasised it again now in his kiss. It was a kiss of fire, white-hot and burning, stamping the brand of his possession on her lips in a way that made her blood run molten in her veins in equally heated response. In the moment that their mouths met and locked and fused, all her senses woke and sang in soaring reaction in Cesare's lightest touch and she knew that she was lost. That no other man had ever made her feel like this, and that if, for now, this was all that Cesare could give her then for now she would let it be enough.

But somewhere way down, in the furthest, deepest part of her soul, a small, lonely voice, lost and forlorn, cried that it was not enough. That she needed more and without it she would starve, emotionally.

But Cesare had lifted his head, his hand had closed firmly around hers, warm and hard and possessive as his kiss. The moment was gone, time moved on, the marriage service taking the usual path to its conclusion. In a daze she followed her husband's lead, moving with him to the vestry, signing the register where she was told, though her eyes would barely focus on what she was writing. All she was conscious of was the bold, firm slash of her husband's signature, hard and confident and sure as the man himself.

Cesare Santorino. And below it, slightly shaky and far less assertive in every way, her own name, Megan Ellis, for the last time.

'Congratulations, Mrs Santorino,' someone said, and automatically she looked round, searching for some sight of the woman being addressed because she had understood that, only just out of hospital after an appendix operation, Cesare's mother had decided against travelling to England for the wedding.

'Where…?' she began then belatedly realised that the registrar who had spoken was holding his hand out to her. That *she* was the Mrs Santorino he was speaking to.

And suddenly that *Mrs* made the ground frighteningly unsteady beneath her feet, the down-to-earth English term hitting home in a way that Cesare's Italian had not.

She was *Mrs Santorino*!

The blood leached from her cheeks, her legs took on the consistency of cotton wool, her head swam, her stomach clenched painfully. If Cesare hadn't seen her sudden pallor, the way she swayed where she stood, she might have actually given into the weakness she felt and fallen, fainting to the ground.

But he had been watching her like a hawk since the moment they had kissed out there in the church and he saw the change in her face, the way her eyes clouded, the lost and frightened look on her face. And suddenly he was there at her side, his strong fingers coming round her elbow, supporting her until he could tuck her hand under his arm and hold it there. Almost seamlessly he covered her nervous hesitation by putting out his own hand to take the registrar's, which Megan had dazedly ignored until now, shaking it firmly and switching on a warm, appreciative smile.

'I think my wife's a little overwrought,' he inserted easily, squeezing Megan's arm against the hard wall of his ribcage under the perfect fit of his sleek, grey morning coat. 'It's all been rather too much for her—especially when she's been feeling rather delicate just lately.'

'Of course.'

The registrar nodded smiling understanding.

'I usually find that the ladies get more nervous about these events than their husbands do. Pre-wedding nerves and all that. And there is always such a lot to arrange beforehand with a wedding, especially with one that had to be organised as quickly as this one did. It must have been quite a whirlwind romance.'

'On the contrary.' Cesare's tone was as smooth as his smile. 'Megan and I have known each other for years. It's just that when she finally decided to take the plunge, she didn't want to hang about. And as I'd already waited years for her to realise the way I felt about her, I was more than happy to go along with her preference for a very short engagement.'

And as I'd already waited years for her to realise the way I felt about her...

Megan didn't know which hurt most. The lie or the ready ease with which Cesare produced it, the smooth confidence that gave it a false, dishonest ring of truth.

'"I was more than happy to go along with her preference for a very short engagement",' she repeated in a bitter undertone when the registrar was once again out of earshot. 'And I'll just bet he'll have no trouble in working out exactly what was behind that particular remark! I don't know why you didn't just go ahead and tell him I was pregnant, and that was why we were dashing to the altar in this decidedly unseemly haste.'

The look Cesare turned on her was cold to the point of glacial, something that only incensed Megan further. After all, he was the one who had engaged in the 'all men together' bonding, the 'nudge, nudge' hint of 'she just couldn't keep her hands off me' in his tone.

'They're going to have to know the truth sooner or later, Megan. You won't be able to keep that slim-line figure for many more weeks. In a very short time, your condition will start to show, and then people are going to start counting on their fingers and coming to the natural conclusion.'

But she had hoped to have a little time before then to try and adjust. To accept what had happened to her and come to terms with it. Everything had happened so fast. It was barely ten weeks since she had been at university, trying to tackle her exam revision in the aftermath of Gary's bombshell that their affair was over; he didn't want to see her any more. Four weeks later, she had first begun to suspect that something was wrong. And after that, there had been weeks of anxiety, of counting the days, of suspecting, but not knowing.

Then in swift succession there had been the painful realisation that she was pregnant. Her mind flinched away from the memory of the day she had gone to confront Gary, the careless way he had tossed his rejection and the truth about his marriage into her face. His final, callous declaration that if she was sensible she'd 'Get rid of the thing' before it messed up her life for ever.

And now here she was, married to a man who didn't love her. Who had made his physical desire for her plain enough and had offered her a cold-blooded marriage of convenience in order to be able to indulge that passion to the full.

And that was the bitterest blow of all, leaving the burning taste of acid in her mouth so that she felt sick and ill. Her insides had still not settled down from the shock she had felt earlier, and the nauseous ache low down in her stomach only added fuel to the already smouldering anger deep inside.

'I don't know why you didn't go the whole hog if you really wanted to make a good job of it—and told him that the baby wasn't yours, but you were prepared to take it on if it meant you could get me into your bed. After all, that's "the truth" as well, isn't it, and if you're so insistent on everyone knowing...'

'Megan, be quiet! This is neither the time nor the place for this.'

Cesare barely lifted his voice above a whisper but it still had enough force to quell her instantly, driving all the fight from her mind and replacing it with a sense of shock at the way she was behaving—and where. She could only be grateful that the others in the vestry—the registrar, the celebrant, her father and the other witnesses—had tactfully moved away for a moment, clearly thinking that the newly-weds needed a little time and space to themselves.

Heaven alone knew what they thought she and Cesare had been talking about! But perhaps, being too distant to be able to hear what had been said, she supposed they might just have thought that their intent concentration on each other, the way they had looked nowhere but into each other's eyes, was the result of deep and loving devotion rather than the angry spat that was the real truth.

But now the priest moved forward, his smile encompassing the two of them equally.

'It's time we went back,' he said easily. If he had suspected anything about the content of their conversation, there was no hint of it in his tone. 'Are you ready?'

'Perfectly,' Cesare assured him, turning to follow and holding out his arm to Megan so that she had no option but to rest her hand on it again, an electric tingle running along every nerve as she felt the strength of bone, the bunch and play of muscle under the fine material of his elegant jacket.

Her mind seemed to split in two, one half of it wanting exactly this. Wanting to hold on tight to Cesare's strength and never let go, to clench her fingers around his arm, feel it support her as it had done moments before. That part begged to allow herself to dream of the way it would feel to have that strength reach out to enclose her, hold her tight. The other, weaker, side of her thoughts only wanted to snatch her hand away and turn and run, away from here, away from the emotional distress she knew she was laying herself open to, the bitter pain of living with and loving a man who didn't feel the same way about her.

Somehow she managed to get through what remained of the ceremony. She went back out into the church, walked by Cesare's side down the long, stone-flagged aisle and out into the bright sunlight of a late July day. She even managed to switch on a smile at the right moment, direct it at the right people. She could only pray that no one saw the emptiness behind the gesture, the way no lightness touched or warmed her eyes but left them cold and dead as the feeling in her soul.

The only time her careful mask faltered was when they were outside the church, every movement accompanied by a chorus of congratulations and a hail of brightly coloured confetti. It was as they were making their way to the car that was to take them to the reception, that someone spoke behind her, their voice carrying loud and clear in a moment of unexpected silence.

'It's been lovely! Really lovely.'

Megan recognised the tones of her father's secretary, a stout, middle-aged lady with an incurably romantic streak.

'If you ask me, it's been a dream wedding.'

A dream wedding. The words fixed themselves inside Megan's head as the car moved, began to pull away from the crowd gathered by the kerb. The sight of Annie Patrick's broad, handsome face half hidden behind a flowery handkerchief as the older woman dabbed at her tearful eyes with obvious enjoyment, only added to and aggravated her feeling of isolation and loss.

In some ways it was true: this was her dream wedding. It was the wedding she had fantasised about as an adolescent, the images clear in her mind as she fell asleep in the narrow single bed in her father's house. The setting was the same, the groom at her side was the man she had always pictured as her husband in those long-ago daydreams. But the details of the circumstances in which they were getting married, the reasons for the wedding at all, were such a bitter irony that they turned her dream wedding into a black, dark nightmare.

'If you're going to wear that expression all day long, then no one is going to believe in the image of this as a whirlwind romance and a happy ever after wedding,' Cesare reproved sharply as he leaned back against the soft leather of the seat of the antique Rolls Royce. 'You look more like someone who's on the way to her execution rather than the excited young bride about to embark on a lifetime of married bliss.'

'Maybe that's because that perfectly describes the way I feel!' Megan returned tartly, refusing to look at him but concentrating her attention on the bouquet of roses in her lap, blinking furiously to drive back the tears that welled unexpectedly. 'We both know that this wedding is a farce—the marriage nothing but a pretence, and a bad one at that!'

'Well then maybe you'd better buck your ideas up—and fast! If you wander around with that scowl on your face then people are pretty soon going to guess...'

'Perhaps I want them to guess!'

This time she turned to face him, yellow flames of defiance flaring in her eyes.

'Did you ever think of that?'

'And did you ever think of your father in all this?' Cesare stunned her by returning, an edge of something dangerous in his voice.

If Tom suspected this marriage wasn't for real there was no knowing what he'd do. He was quite capable of backing out, refusing the help he so desperately needed. And if her father backed out, then possibly Megan would too.

'Dad? What has he got to do with this?'

'If I remember rightly, a rescue deal for your father was part of the bargain between us when we arranged all this.'

Cesare's tone was hard, unyielding, totally ruthless.

'As soon as we were married, you said!' Megan put in protestingly. Surely he couldn't be thinking of backing out now!

'But only if people believe that this is a real marriage. One hint of anyone suspecting that there's nothing in it— that it's not the love match it appears to be, then the deal's off.'

Was he really threatening to back out now? To refuse to help her—and her father after all? Surely he couldn't be so cruel!

But then she looked into his dark, set face and knew that *this* Cesare Santorino, the man his business opponents must come up against so often across a boardroom table, could easily be so cruel. He could be all that and more.

'But that isn't fair!' she protested. 'It wasn't in our original agreement!'

'But I'm putting it in there now.'

Cesare's tone left no room for argument or remonstration.

'If you want I'll have a legal document drawn up to say exactly that.'

Knowing she was defeated, Megan subsided again, staring fixedly at her bouquet.

'There's no need for that. You've got the whip hand and you know it.'

'The whip hand?' Cesare questioned, his near-perfect English deserting him momentarily.

'You're in the driving seat—in control,' she elaborated unwillingly, tugging off a leaf in the bouquet and discarding it on the floor of the car. 'You've got me exactly where you want me and I have to do as you say or you'll just drop me right in it.'

Did she really think that? Cesare was forced to wonder. Did she really think that this was nothing but a power struggle? A battle for control where one of them must win and so the other must, inevitably, be the loser? Couldn't she see that there was a way they could both end up the winner? If she could stop throwing the fact that she'd been forced into this marriage in his face; if she'd stop thinking about what might have been with Gary and let herself consider what *could be* between the two of them; if she'd only let him *in* in some way, then things could be very different.

But looking at her now, with her head bent, her face determinedly turned away from him, it was clear she was determined to shut him out, rather than let him in. Her slender hands moved restlessly on the beautiful bouquet, pulling at a leaf here, a petal there, the movement betraying the inner turmoil of her thoughts.

'Megan…'

Reaching forward, he placed a hand on hers, stilling the nervous movements. Instantly he felt her tense, the muscles in her hand and arm clenching tight, making him regret his action even before he had finally completed it.

Did she really find his touch so offensive? Did she still wish, even after his callous rejection of her, the betrayal of her trust that his seduction of her had been, that bloody *Gary* was the one in the car with her now? That it was Gary's ring she wore on her finger, Gary's name she had taken as her own?

Just the thought of the other man changed his mood in an instant. Anger boiled up, thick and hot. Anger at Rowell for the way he had behaved, at Megan for clinging on to a hope of something she could never have; something that had never existed in the first place. But most of all he was furious with himself for *caring*; for wanting it all to be different.

He and Megan were alike in this at least, he admitted to himself. Both searching for a dream that would never be theirs. He was as crazy, as foolish as she was. He had her in his life; she would be in his home, in his day-to-day existence, in his *bed*. Couldn't he be satisfied with that? Why did he have to go and want her heart as well?

But he had never been one to settle for second best, and he didn't plan on starting now.

'Megan…' he said again and the new note of steel brought her head up in a rush, green eyes widening swiftly as she looked into his face.

For a moment her soft lips parted as if she was about to say something but then immediately she clearly reconsidered and closed her mouth again, waiting in silence for him to speak.

To her total confusion, Cesare leaned forward and rapped

firmly on the glass partition that divided their part of the car from the uniformed driver.

'Pull over here and park for a minute,' he ordered crisply. 'Then take a minute to stretch your legs—get some air.'

'Cesare!' Megan protested as the chauffeur did as he was told. 'We can't do this! We're expected at the reception any minute. Everyone will be coming along behind us. They'll expect us to be there...'

'We can do what the hell we want. If we're not there, they'll wait for us. Whoever heard of a wedding reception going ahead without the bride and groom?'

'But...' Megan tried again and he laid a finger across her lips to silence her.

'No talking—this time you listen! I think you'd better decide right here and now if you want this show of marriage to work or not. Because if you do, then you're going to have to work a lot harder on looking as if you actually believe in what you're doing. If you insist on going around with a face like—what is it you say?—like a wet weekday?'

'Weekend,' Megan supplied automatically, unable to hold back a faint smile at his rare stumble in his use of English.

It was shocking how much it affected her, touching her numbed heart and warming it slightly. Cesare had always seemed so very sure of himself, so capable and confident. Even this tiny slip made him seem so much more human, even the faintest bit vulnerable, and it was not a sensation she was used to.

'The phrase is a wet weekend.'

'Okay...'

Cesare shrugged off her mild correction.

'But whatever the phrase is, that is how you look. And as everyone knows it is not the way that a bride should look on her wedding day. You should look as if all your dreams had come true; as if there was nothing more in the world that you could hope for.'

He caught her sidelong glance and an expression that was half smile, half scowl, crossed his face in response.

'Okay, so there is no room for such feelings in our relationship,' he growled bad-temperedly. 'But you could at least damn well smile!'

Deliberately Megan switched on a blatantly false smile, all teeth and lips, nothing in the eyes. And, as she expected, Cesare's frown grew darker.

'I can't do it!' she protested. 'Unless, of course you could help.'

'Help? How?'

Megan would never know what little extra infusion of courage gave her the nerve to try it. But suddenly she was leaning towards him, bringing her face close to his, looking into his eyes.

'If you behaved like a bridegroom, then I might find it easier to act as a bride.'

The deep brown eyes were full of suspicion and also, Megan was stunned to see, a tiny shadow of wary uncertainty lurked in their depths.

'And how, *adorata*, should your groom behave?'

'Well…'

Her voice threatened to abandon her and she swallowed convulsively to ease the dryness in her throat.

'You could try kissing me, for example.'

The swift, slanting look he directed at her seemed to be full of reproof, taking her heart and twisting it painfully in response.

'No, of course not!'

In a fury of embarrassment she turned away again, looking down at her bouquet, out of the window, anywhere but into that dark, unreadable face.

'Megan…'

His voice was very low, very soft but she refused to respond to it, keeping her head stubbornly averted.

But then a hand, warm and firm, came under her chin, closing on her delicate jaw with a clasp that was gentle but irresistible and turning her face back to his.

'*Un bacio*…' he murmured, soft and warm as melted honey.

And it was the sweetest kiss she had ever received. The most gentle, tender taking of her lips she had known in her lifetime. It made her heart sing, woke her soul, opened her heart to the possibilities of endless dreams. And it stirred her senses too, with the promise of the joys of loving, the yearning delight of passion and the final, total culmination of desire.

It seemed to go on and on for ever, and yet it could never have lasted long enough to satisfy her. And when he finally released her she was incapable of speech, of thought. She could only sink back in her seat, her thoughts swimming on a heated golden sea, the taste of him still strong on her mouth.

But then at last Cesare moved, lifting his hand to summon the driver and the magical moment splintered all around them, threatening to break Megan's heart all over again as it did so. Hastily she tried to compose herself, to prepare for the continuation of their journey to the country-house hotel where their reception was to be held.

She hadn't expected Cesare to speak and so when he leaned forward and took her hand she jumped like a startled cat, turning wide, uncertain eyes on his unsmiling face.

'So tell me, *moglie mia*,' he asked, still in those honeyed tones. 'Was that what you were looking for? Was that the way to make you feel like a bride—to make you smile?'

The light in her eyes was answer enough, but still she

had to put it into words, had to speak just a little of what was in her heart or she knew she would burst under the strain of holding it in.

'Oh yes,' she said, clasping his fingers as tightly as she dared, the smile he was looking for curving her lips, wide and true, if just a little tremulous at the edges. 'Yes, Cesare, oh yes. That was exactly what I needed!'

CHAPTER SIX

'ALONE at last!'

Cesare sighed and stretched; flexing tight muscles under the smooth material of the silver-grey suit he had changed into before they had left the hotel. 'I thought they'd never let us go.'

Megan could only nod mutely in agreement, unable to find any words to answer him.

Alone at last. She had known that this time must come, that inevitably, by the end of the day, all their family and friends would depart and she would be left alone with this man who was now her husband, but somehow nothing had quite prepared her for the finality of the moment. And now that it was here, she had no idea at all how to handle it.

All day she had been a prey to huge fluctuations of mood. One moment her heart had been clenching in fear at the thought of the sheer enormity of what she had done, the prospect of just what she had committed herself to. The next, she had been fizzing with happiness, her mind aglow with delight at the thought that she and Cesare were now husband and wife.

Okay, so things were very far from perfect. They had a long, long way to go before they could say they had reached any real understanding—and 'understanding' was an even longer way from the 'happy ever after' she had dreamed of having with Cesare. But they were together. And with care and hard work and rather more than just a pinch of luck, one day, they might just reach that special wonderful goal.

She was prepared to put in that hard work anyway. And she was beginning to suspect that perhaps Cesare was too.

'Tired?'

Her new husband's question was low and sympathetic and the look he turned on her blended concern with understanding in a way that had the tears pricking at her eyes again.

Another mood swing, she thought shakily, disturbed by the suddennes of it. One moment up, feet off the floor in happiness, the next plunging down to something close to despair and panic. Probably caused by her hormones, she told herself, knowing how she had often felt just before her period started and assuming that pregnancy must have very much the same effect.

'It's been a long day,' she managed, and he nodded agreement.

'A long day but I think everything went off all right. No one seemed to suspect anything was other than as we'd said.'

They'd planned carefully just what they would tell their families. What explanation they would give for the suddenness of their marriage plans.

'We'll tell them we've always felt this way about each other,' Cesare had said. 'But we've kept quiet about it because each of us suspected that the other didn't feel the same way. But after the party at New Year, we just couldn't keep it to ourselves any longer. We've been seeing each other since then—while you were away at university. That will explain why the baby will come "early". They're bound to suspect something like that anyway.'

'We can hardly avoid it,' Megan had put in. 'Even with a very speedy wedding, the birth's going to be no more than seven months away.'

'Then we'll be totally upfront about it. Tell them we

realised we'd wasted years already and now we didn't want to wait any longer—for the marriage or anything else.'

It was near enough the truth, Cesare thought now. On his side at least. It was just with Megan that the story was pure fiction from start to finish. But perhaps, given time, he could change that.

'I didn't like deceiving my father, but in the end I don't suppose he'll mind.'

The truth was that her father had amazed her with his lack of surprise at their announcement of their immediate marriage plans. Perhaps it was because Cesare had already said something to him about helping him out of the financial disaster he had got himself into.

Certainly, Tom Ellis had seemed like a different person at the wedding reception. He'd walked several inches taller, his spine straighter, his shoulders looking as if they'd had a major weight taken off them. There had been a new light in his eyes and a ready smile on his lips and he'd laughed out loud several times—a sound she had once wondered if she would ever hear again.

'He'll adjust—like my parents will adjust to becoming in-laws and grandparents almost all at once.'

'I hope so…'

She only wished she could feel as confident as he sounded. Cesare had said that he would be a father to her baby, had declared that it would be as if Gary had never existed—but could he really do that? Could he truly push the other man's existence and his part in the making of the baby out of his mind and act as if it truly was his child, and his parents' grandchild?

At the thought, her stomach, which had been decidedly untrustworthy all day, lurched nauseously, making her feel even more uncomfortable than before. Her head ached and her back did too and surreptitiously she rubbed it with the back of her hand.

'You look pale.'

Cesare didn't miss a trick.

'Are you sure you're feeling okay?'

'I'm tired,' she admitted. 'But then I think anyone would be after such an eventful day.'

But perhaps someone whose wedding had been the real thing—a genuine love match—wouldn't feel quite so worn down and deflated by the end of the day. A couple who truly loved each other would be feeling their very best right now, delighted to have reached the end of the day so that they could be alone together. They might be tired but they would be buzzing with excitement, anticipating the best part of their wedding that was to happen when they finally went to bed.

They wouldn't be eyeing each other uncertainly, nerves taut as violin strings, wondering just how the other person felt and wondering what was to come for the rest of the evening.

'Yes, they would,' Cesare agreed. 'And you're not exactly on top form.'

'I'm pregnant, Cesare, not ill!'

Uncomfortably aware of the undercurrents beneath what he was saying, the coded message that threaded through his words, she snapped at him bad-temperedly then immediately wished the words back.

'Lots of women cope with more than this and still manage.'

'But you look worn out. I just wanted to make sure you weren't overdoing things.'

Megan had to bite down hard on her lower lip, fighting against the impulse to scream, to demand to know why he didn't just come right out and say it. She knew that what he was really saying was, are you *too* tired? Or are you ready for tonight? For our *wedding night*?

Are you ready to go to bed with me?

And she knew what her answer would be.

It would be *yes.*

It had to be yes. It couldn't be anything else.

Of course she was ready to go to bed with him; to make love to him. There was no room for doubt, or hesitation, in her mind. It was what she wanted—what she had always wanted, almost all her life, it seemed. She loved Cesare and she wanted to make love with him. The sex wasn't the problem.

Telling him was.

She couldn't just blurt it out right here and now, opening her mouth and stating it boldly and frankly, in the way that she felt it deep inside. That was what she had tried to do at New Year—and her insides still curdled at the thought.

At New Year she had spilled out what was in her heart to Cesare and he had just laughed at her and walked away. She couldn't bear it if that was to happen now. Not on her wedding day. Not when they had already started out in such an inauspicious manner and she wanted—needed—so desperately to put things right between them.

'I've not overdone things, honest.'

Drawing a deep breath she decided to take a risk, mentally closing her eyes and plunging right in.

'And I've had a lovely, lovely day.'

That took him by surprise, bringing his dark head round to her in shock.

But, 'I'm glad you enjoyed it,' was all he said.

'Oh I did!'

She refused to let his carefully guarded delivery, the total lack of emotion in his voice get to her. He wasn't anything like as indifferent and controlled as he sounded. He might have thought that he had played his cards very very close to his chest all day but there had been moments when his command over his behaviour had slipped and the result had been some of the best, the most special moments of the day.

There had been several of those magical times, ones she had hugged to herself secretly, not wanting anyone else to know just how much they had meant to her.

The first had been the moment when they had arrived at the reception and she had been wondering just what she should do with the glass of champagne she had been handed, thinking she would have to try and tip it away somewhere without being seen. Cesare had whisked the glass away from her and replaced it with another filled with an apparently identical liquid.

'Apple juice and sparkling water,' he'd explained casually. 'Has exactly the same sparkle and fizz, but there's nothing in there to harm our secret.'

He'd been there for her throughout the event, always checking she was all right. It had seemed as if every single time she looked up she met Cesare's thoughtful gaze, the ebony eyes watching every move, observing everything she did. He had been there if she looked tired or uncertain, or just a little in need of support, appearing at her side as if by magic and spiriting her away to a quiet part of the room until she felt ready to face people again.

And they had danced together too. As the first waltz of the evening was announced, along with the words, 'Ladies and gentlemen, I give you Mr and Mrs Santorino', Cesare had taken her hand in his and led her onto the dance floor. He had kept her close throughout the dance, holding her as carefully and as tenderly as he had kissed her in the car on the way back from the church and, as a result, any last wariness in her heart had melted away for ever. Her feet had barely seemed to touch the floor as she danced, and she had locked her eyes with his, aware of nothing but his deep, dark gaze, holding her mesmerised. The sounds, the colour, the other people at the reception had all faded away into a hazy blur at the edge of her consciousness, and it had been as if there was only her and Cesare, alone in all the world, and that was just the way she wanted it.

And then tonight, when they had reached his home just outside London where they were to spend their first night, he had stunned her even more.

They had arrived at the house as the evening finally gathered in, and he had dismissed the chauffeur with a word of thanks and what was obviously a very generous tip.

'We'll stay here tonight,' he had explained, 'but tomorrow our proper honeymoon will begin.'

Seeing her start of surprise, his mouth had twisted cynically.

'You didn't think I'd forget an important detail like a honeymoon did you?'

'Not forget, no. But I didn't think that really a honeymoon was—appropriate—to this marriage.'

'Everything that's *appropriate* to any other marriage is *appropriate* to ours, Megan.'

The black cynicism with which he echoed her own use of the word made Megan flinch inside.

'I only meant…'

'I know exactly what you meant,' Cesare snapped, his tone even harsher than before. 'But you'd better rethink your ideas—fast. I don't give a damn how you feel about it, but as far as I'm concerned this marriage of ours is as real as any other. There's no turning back now, *cara*. We're married, and that's how it's going to stay.'

'I—I know…' Megan began but he rushed on, heedless of her stumbling interjection.

'I didn't just go through that wedding for show—I meant every word I said in those vows. You're my wife, and I'm your husband, and if anyone begins to suspect anything there'll be hell to pay.'

Megan could only nod, still stunned by the fierce possessiveness with which he had said those emotive words, 'You're my wife'. But even as she was still absorbing them, he continued, rocking her sense of reality once more.

'And we'll observe every tradition, every rite of the whole occasion—even this one...'

And while she was still registering just what he had said, he had unlocked and pushed open the front door, turning back to her to fold his arms around her, swing her off her feet and high up into the air.

'Cesare!'

Her breath escaped from her lungs in a shocked, bewildered gasp and she clutched at his broad shoulders, fearful she might fall. But his hands came under her knees, supported her back, his strength taking the weight of her body easily. All she could do was cling on and go with what he wanted as he carried her across the threshold and into the wide, tiled hallway beyond.

Even now, she still trembled deep inside at just the memory of the sensations that had coursed through her in those moments. The way that her heart had lurched into a crazy, staccato beat, sending the blood rushing round her body until her head was spinning in an uncontrolled delight.

And once inside, as he'd finally lowered her to the floor, he had deliberately let her body slide slowly down the lean, powerful length of his; legs, hips, and finally breasts all coming into the most intimate contact with every inch of him. And because of that it had been totally impossible to ignore the swollen physical evidence of his heated response to her closeness, the instant desire he made no attempt to hide.

It was there in the kiss that followed too. In the way that he had taken her lips with a burning, demanding force that spoke of hunger and passion, and the deep, deep sensuality of the night, all combined with the promise that he would make this a time she would never forget. And she had answered that promise with one of her own, kissing him right back with all the strength and the emotion she was capable of feeling.

'I *want* you,' he had said. 'I want you more than life itself. I always have and I always will.' And simply remembering the dark intensity with which he had spoken those words made her shiver as matching sensations fizzed over her skin, sparking electrical storms of response along each tingling nerve.

'And it's not over yet—our wedding day, I mean.'

It was as close as she dared come to saying exactly what was in her heart, the stinging excitement that ran through her at just the thought of what was to come.

'But I think I would feel better if I could freshen up—draw breath, take a shower.'

'Of course. Your cases were brought over earlier, so everything you need is upstairs.'

He led her up the great curving staircase and into an enormous room decorated in tones of green, light and dark, a huge bay window overlooking the park-size garden at the back of the house.

'The bathroom's through there...'

He indicated a door leading off at the far side of the room.

'There are fresh towels there and everything you should need. But if you want anything, just give a shout.'

'Mmm.'

It was all that she could manage. The sight of the king-size bed, big, like everything else in this man's life, had dried her throat painfully, closing it up against any words.

Yes, she might tell herself that she wanted him as much as he wanted her. And she might feel excited at the anticipation at what was to come between them. But that anticipation was mixed with a shivering tension that gripped her harder when confronted with the reality of the place where it was to happen. With the bed in which Cesare would take her, make her his. Now she truly did feel as nervous and unsure of herself as any virgin bride on her wedding night.

Would excitement be enough? Would the passion that flared between them when they kissed carry her through and into the fulfilment and the pleasure that sexual intimacy was supposed to bring? She felt that it would. Instinct told her that with Cesare she would find that satisfaction. Because the truth was that with Gary she had never even come close.

His lovemaking had been uninspiring, to say the least. In fact she had been so disturbed by her own lack of response that she had been forced to wonder if there was something wrong with her. Now, her suspicions were of the opposite. That in fact he had not taken the trouble to arouse her, or give her any real enjoyment.

Which left her totally unsure of how she could react to the man she loved.

'You'll feel more comfortable if you get out of your finery and into something more relaxed.' Cesare was still totally concerned with practicalities. 'Take your time about everything.'

'Thank you.'

He was heading for the door but suddenly he paused and swung back, dark eyes going straight to her face.

'Did I tell you that you looked beautiful today? More

than that—you looked stunning. I was so proud when I saw you walking down the aisle towards me.'

'And I was proud to be walking to you,' Megan managed though her voice croaked embarrassingly.

Why did he just stand there, keeping a distance between them? The width of the carpet might be only a metre or two, but the expanse of it seemed as huge and unbrideable as if they were on either side of the Grand Canyon, totally unable to reach the other side. If only he would touch her, hold her...

She tried to will him to do so in her thoughts, struggling to telegraph wordless messages to him with her eyes, but he seemed totally impervious to her unsettled mood.

'So is there anything else you need?'

'N-no. I think I have everything.'

It couldn't be further from the truth. What she truly needed was for him to take her in his arms and hold her tight. She longed for him to caress her, kiss her senseless, to drive away all the fears and uncertainties she was a prey to and replace them with the yearning, aching, shivering hunger that had taken her over that day in the library. Then she had been unable to think but only to *feel*. And she wanted to experience all those sensations over again.

But clearly Cesare thought that he was being considerate. That he was showing a patience and sensitivity he thought she needed. And she didn't have the nerve to tell him he couldn't be more wrong.

'Then I'll leave you in peace.'

'Thank you.'

Disappointment made it stiff and tight. A disappointment that grew deeper and more bitter as she watched him walk away from her again. But the memory of the way he had rejected her at the New Year party was clear and cruelly sharp in her mind, coming between her and any attempt to try and call him back.

This was supposed to be their wedding night. The night when they consummated their relationship by making love with each other. But Cesare's attitude had made it painfully plain that in his mind there wasn't a relationship to consummate at all. He had declared that he wanted her physically and that hunger had been enough to drive him to marry her, but there was nothing else, nothing emotional for him to offer her at all.

Sighing miserably, she kicked off her shoes and padded over the soft carpet towards the bathroom. She really needed this shower to make her feel human again. Her back ached terribly and her stomach was raw and tender.

'*Porca miseria*!' Cesare cursed to himself as he made his way down the stairs. Would he ever get it right?

He had wanted to take everything so carefully. Give her time to adjust. But it seemed that she still regarded him as the enemy. As someone she feared and didn't trust. Would he ever live down the way he had behaved at New Year?

Reaching the living room, he headed straight for the drinks cabinet, then immediately paused, the bottle of red wine in his hands.

'That's not the way, you fool!'

That had been his mistake on New Year's Eve. Determined to stick strictly to his promise to her father, he had had one glass—okay, more than one glass, too many, in the hope of distracting himself from the way she looked. It hadn't worked. If anything, it had made matters worse. The alcohol had heightened every one of his senses, bringing them into painfully sharp awareness of the brilliant beauty of her hair and eyes, the delicate texture of her skin, the slim lines of her body in the clinging gold slip of a dress. Even just to think of the scent she had been wearing made

his body harden, demanding to bury itself in the warm softness of her feminine body and abandon itself to the delights
of loving her.

'*Dio*!' he muttered again, furious with himself and with
the circumstances he had found himself trapped in.

If only her birthday had been earlier in the year. Either
that or her father had made the term of his promise last
until her twenty-first birthday, not her twenty-second.

But Tom had married Barbara on the day she had turned
twenty and he blamed all the unhappiness of his marriage
on that simple fact. His wife had been too young to know
her own mind, he had said. She had never really lived,
never enjoyed herself, never known any true freedom.
Within six months she had been pregnant with Megan and
she had felt trapped by motherhood and domesticity. Before
her daughter was ten years old, she had walked out on her
marriage and her child, looking for the freedom she thought
she was owed and breaking Tom Ellis's heart for ever in
the process.

'I was too old for Barbara—or she was too young for
me,' Tom had said when, unable to hold back any longer,
Cesare had blurted out the intensity of his feelings for his
friend's daughter. 'Either way, we messed up our relationship and made each other desperately unhappy. I want better than that for my Meggie.'

He'd wanted better for her too, Cesare told himself, kick-
ing a chair out of the way as he paced up and down the
elegant room, trying to find a way to fill in the time until
Megan reappeared. And above all else he'd wanted to make
sure that the relationship he hoped for didn't end up on the
rocks for the same reasons her parents' had done.

And so he'd understood when Tom had asked him to
wait. To at least let Megan have her time at university, and

the freedom and the experiences her mother had been denied, before he had told her of the way he felt.

And he'd managed fine while she was still young enough to find him boringly old and uninteresting, when she had kept her distance. But at Christmas it had been hell on earth keeping to his promise. From the start of the holidays, it had been clear that Megan had changed. She had grown up for one thing, developing from a lovely girl into a beautiful young woman. He hadn't been able to take his eyes off her. And she had known it. She had flirted outrageously with him at every possible opportunity. And then at New Year she had done more than flirt.

She had thrown herself at him. She'd told him that she'd 'fancied him rotten' for years. That there was no one else in the world for her. That she *loved* him. And then she'd enticed him into a quiet, dark corner where she'd flung her arms round him, kissed him until his head was spinning and his loins were throbbing with hot desire. And she'd whispered that they could go to her room. That no one would notice…

Porca miseria! No!

He would drive himself mad if he remembered the fight he had had to resist her. The struggle with his conscience and his promise to her father. That night he *had* turned to the bottle. He'd pushed her away from him. Lied through his teeth to her, telling her that he didn't want her; that he wasn't interested in kids; that he wanted a real woman in his life, not a half-grown baby. It hadn't been kind. In fact, it had been downright cruel, but he hadn't been able to think of any other way to escape from her and still hold true to the promise he had made to her father.

And then he'd gone home and got desperately, stupidly, totally drunk. It hadn't helped.

And it wouldn't help now. Because tonight he had to

remain perfectly sober. He had to be completely in control and able to function at his best. Because tonight he was going to start the campaign to win Megan back from that *bastardo* Rowell.

Tonight he was going to make love to Megan with all the skill, all the finesse, and all the gentleness he could manage. He was going to seduce her, entice her into his bed, strip all the clothes from her body, and then he was going to kiss her all over. Press his mouth to every perfect inch of her. He was going to awaken every sensual nerve in her body, caress her until she was delirious with pleasure, incapable of thought, and begging him to take her—*now*! And when he did make love to her he was going to make sure that he erased all thought of Gary Rowell from her mind. That he would drive her to such ecstasies that she would only ever have room for him in her mind and she would never—*never*—think of her former lover again.

Dannazione. He had sworn that he would wait, but he couldn't take any more. He had to be with her; had to see her again. Surely she had finished her shower by now.

Striding from the room, he mounted the stairs two at a time, pushing open the bedroom door in a rush of uncontrolled enthusiasm.

'Megan, I...'

She wasn't there. The room was still empty; the door to the bathroom still closed. But the shower had been switched off and no sound of running water reached him through the door.

Bene! She would be out soon. All he had to do was wait. But first...

The jeweller's box was in the top drawer of the dresser. Taking it out, Cesare opened it and checked the contents then cast a searching glance around the room.

He wanted somewhere where she wouldn't find it at once

but where—just at the right moment—he could reach for
it.

With a small sound of satisfaction he smoothed the soft,
downy feather pillows on what would be Megan's side of
the bed and placed the small box carefully on the top of
them. Then he sat down on the edge of the bed and waited.

And waited.

Still she didn't come and after a few minutes he felt
restless again, this time mixed with a disturbing sense of
unease.

'Megan!' he called, pitching his voice so that it would
carry through the wood of the door. 'Are you all right?'

'Mmm…' She sounded unsettled, distracted. 'Just give
me a minute.'

Smiling to himself, Cesare settled back again. Nerves, he
told himself. And that had to be a good sign. Very probably
it meant that the rat Rowell hadn't been much of a lover.
Well, he'd soon put that right. He'd show Megan just what
making love was really like. He'd woo her, and he'd win
her…

If only she would come out of that damn bathroom!

'Megan!'

Getting to his feet he moved rapidly across the room,
rattled at the door handle.

'Megan! What the hell are you doing!'

No, impatience was a bad idea. He didn't want to
frighten her. Didn't want to make her any more nervous
than she already was.

Forcing himself back to sit on the bed, he looked at the
jewellery box again and frowned, dissatisfied. Lifting the
pillows, he pushed the gift out of sight underneath.

As he did so, his hands tangled in the delicate ivory silk
and lace that formed the flimsy, sexy garment that would

be laughingly described as a night*gown* and his smile grew wider, more sensually satisfied.

Why had she bought the enticing thing, if not because she wanted to feel sexy when she was with him? Because she wanted to please him, tantalise him—seduce him too.

The thought was so delightful, so exciting, that when he heard the jerky slide of the bolt, the door opening behind him, he turned, eager as a boy, longing to see the one, the only love of his life.

He knew that something was terribly wrong as soon as he looked into her face. If he had thought she looked worn and pale earlier, then she was ashen now. Washed out and colourless. Even worse than she had looked that night in the library when she had told him how appallingly Rowell had treated her.

Shocked and stunned, he lurched to his feet and started forwards, his hands coming out to support her as she swayed weakly in the doorway, clutching the pale-green towel to her.

'Meggie—what is it?' he demanded. 'Tell me...'

'Cesare! Help me!' she interrupted, her voice wobbling desperately, her eyes wide dark pools above the whiteness of her cheeks. 'Get a doctor, please—and quickly! Something's very, very wrong. I'm—I'm *bleeding*!'

CHAPTER SEVEN

FROM the appalling, terrifying moment in which she'd realised just what was happening to her, Megan's mind had become just a scream of terror so that everything that happened did so in a blur of fear, nothing but the horror of her discovery making any impact on her thoughts.

She was hardly aware of stumbling to the door and wrenching it open, knowing only that she had to find Cesare. That she had to be with him, beg him to help her. He would know what to do.

And he did. He didn't waste a second phoning for a doctor, using his phone instead to summon the chauffeur even as he bundled her up in a black towelling robe that he snatched from the back of the bedroom door in the same moments that he snapped orders into the receiver. And as he fastened it round her, pulling the belt around her waist, he had soothed and comforted her with a non-stop flow of gentle words.

'Hold on, *cara*,' he'd urged. 'Don't panic. We're on our way. Everything's going to be fine. I'll take care of you. Just hold on to me. Hold tight. I'll make sure that you're okay.'

Megan had wished that she could believe him. That she could hope and trust that things would indeed be 'fine'. But the tearing discomfort deep inside, the terrible feeling of nausea, told its own story. There wasn't a chance that she was still pregnant. She knew that for sure.

But still there was a deep, primitive comfort to be gained from being in Cesare's arms, and being wrapped in the soft, thick towelling of his robe. It wrapped around her almost twice, it was so loose; and it smelled wonderfully of his skin and the cologne he used so that she could almost believe he had only just taken it off in order to wrap it about her. Whimpering in pain and misery, she huddled into its warmth and abandoned herself to Cesare's total control.

She was barely aware of the way that he swept her off her feet and carried her out to the waiting car. The speeding, swaying journey passed in a haze of discomfort and fear and it was only the strength of Cesare's arms around her, the sound of his voice in her ear, that kept her from screaming aloud in distress and panic. As it was, she had to clamp her teeth down hard on her bottom lip in order to hold back the sobs and all the time tears poured down her cheeks, silent and unstoppable, scouring wet, desolate trails over her colourless skin.

At the hospital there was none of the delay she had expected and feared. Once again Cesare took charge and bulldozed ruthlessly over anyone who got in his way or tried to suggest anything other than he wanted.

He didn't wait, he didn't ask, instead he insisted loud and clear on getting exactly what he wanted. He wanted the best, the most comfortable room. They were taken there at once. He wanted the most qualified doctor—the senior gynaecologist—and the leading expert appeared at a run. He demanded the best possible treatment, the newest, most advanced help—and they promised him she would have everything they could provide.

But all the equipment, all the expertise in the world couldn't help. Nothing could stop the bleeding. Nothing could prevent what was happening. They could only give her something to ease the pain and then wait and watch and let nature take its course. There was no going back and they could only bow to the inevitable.

And then, late on the following morning, when Megan finally woke from the shattered, exhausted sleep into which she had fallen at the end of a long, long, desolate night, the doctor came to see her and she learned that fate had one last final, terrible shock in store for her. The worst bolt from the blue that she could ever have imagined.

She hadn't lost her baby because she had never had one to lose. She wasn't pregnant at all. Never had been. It had all just been a figment of her imagination, a creation of her mind and not her body. It had been a phantom pregnancy. A fiction. A delusion.

'But I did a test!' she wailed, unable to take the full horror of it in. 'It was positive!'

She could only be grateful that the consultant had chosen a time when Cesare wasn't at her side as he had been all night. After a long, sleepless night, he had finally been prevailed on to go home and get some rest. His wife was in no danger, they had assured him. What she needed now was to sleep, and so did he. They would call him if anything happened.

'The over the counter tests aren't always one hundred per cent accurate,' she was told. 'There's always the risk of a small possibility of error and it looks as if that was what happened this time.'

'But I felt so sick—and I missed my periods! Two of them.'

'And that's probably why you've been in so much discomfort this time. Anything could cause that. Any emotional upset, or not eating properly could easily affect your regular pattern. Had you been under any sort of strain?'

'You could say that,' Megan muttered bitterly. 'I was in the middle of my final exams.'

At the same time as she had found out that her lover was already married. That he had a wife and two children living in America, and that he had been playing her for a total fool. Taking her virginity without a qualm and using her as a sexual diversion to while away the time during his stay in England, fully intending to drop her and go back to his wife just as soon as the term of his exchange was up in the summer.

In fact her only appeal to him had been that virginity. He had seen her innocence as a challenge he was determined to conquer, the taking of it a trophy—a score mark he could carve, metaphorically at least, on the dark wooden headboard of his bed.

'I was so sure I was pregnant.'

She still couldn't take it in.

'Our minds are amazing things. They can work wonders—miracles—and they can do the opposite. When we're under stress our minds can make our bodies think something else is happening. I've seen dozens of people who present with every symptom of some illness when in fact there's nothing wrong.'

And while Megan was still struggling with this idea, the doctor had gone on to reassure her. At least, he thought he was reassuring her.

'It could be better this way. Your husband tells me you're only just married, and perhaps it's better not to be starting out together with a baby on the way in a few months' time. You can have a proper honeymoon, spend time together and enjoy the first weeks of married life free of commitments and other ties. Then later, you can think about having children when you're really ready. I'm sure your husband will understand.'

And that was the worst thing of all.

Perhaps if Cesare truly were her *husband*, then he would understand. If he had married her out of love and because he wanted to spend his life with her, grow old with her, then this set-back, the foolish, naïve mistake she had made, might not matter to him at all.

But her husband wasn't really her husband. He was her husband in name only. He hadn't married her for love but because he believed she was pregnant. With a baby that now no longer existed. A baby that had never existed except in her imagination.

'Do you want me to tell him?' the doctor asked.

'He doesn't know yet?'

Oh, dear God, how was he going to react?

'No—no—let me do it. I'd better tell him. He'll take it better coming from me.'

If only she could believe that. If only there was any way at all that Cesare could take it *better*. But she knew that was impossible. His reaction was going to be as volcanic as the eruption of Mount Etna, no matter what she did or said, and she was going to have to face the consequences of that, even though her heart quailed inside her at just the thought. She owed him that at least. She couldn't leave it to someone else to explain to him.

But the sight of Cesare's face when he came into the room almost destroyed what little was left of her confidence. He might have been sent home to rest, but he had clearly not taken advantage of the opportunity. The stunning brown eyes were heavy and shadowed, and for the first time ever since she had known him his shave was less than perfect. The sight of the tiny red marks on his jaw line, revealing where he had nicked himself in his haste, made Megan's heart twist painfully at the thought of the reasons for his lack of concentration.

'How are you feeling?' he demanded even before he was fully into the room.

'I—I'm okay.'

'And the baby?'

'There—there—I'm afraid there isn't going to be a baby.'

'Oh Megan...'

Coming to the bed, he sat on the side of it, took her hand in both of his.

'I'm so sorry...'

'No!'

She couldn't let it go on like this. Couldn't let him think this way. Her conscience would never give her peace if she did.

'It isn't what you think! It isn't that way at all.'

'Then what way is it?'

She couldn't bear the look in his eyes, the way his dark, intent gaze was fixed on her face, and she stared down at the peach and cream bedspread, studying it as if she was to be tested on describing the pattern later.

'There isn't going to be a baby because—because...'

She swallowed hard, forced herself to go on.

'Because there never was one in the first place.'

It was his stillness that gave him away. The sudden freezing into total immobility that she could sense out of the corners of her eyes.

'I don't understand...'

The ruthless control he was exerting to keep his voice steady showed in the hands that held hers, making them tighten convulsively over her fingers.

'What do you mean there was never one in the first place? Megan...'

It was a note of harsh warning when she couldn't bring herself to answer him.

'Explain!'

Twice she opened her mouth to answer him and both times her voice deserted her. When she finally did force it to work, it was squeaky and breathless, not sounding like her at all.

'There never was a baby in the first place. It seems I wasn't pregnant after all—just deceiving myself.'

'But you went for a test!'

Oh, hell—had he thought she'd meant an official, doctor's test? Of course he had. This was Cesare Santorino. The man who wanted everything signed sealed and copied into triplicate before he committed himself to anything.

'No—I *did* a test. There's a distinct difference. And as it says on the packet there is always the possibility that any result might not be one hundred per cent accurate. They do say that it's wise to get things checked out by a doctor as soon as possible.'

'And am I to take it that you didn't "get things checked out"?'

Megan could only shake her head silently, flinching inside at the savage bitterness of his voice. If he had lost his temper, shouted, screamed at her, she could have understood it. But he didn't. Instead, the question was delivered in a vicious undertone that had all the deadly force of an attacking snake and it was far more damaging because of that.

'Don't you think it would have been wise?'

Her head came up sharply at that, russet hair flying back from her face, green eyes flashing defiance into his cold ebony stare.

'Of course it would have been *wise*—if I'd been thinking straight! But I wasn't, damn you! I wasn't thinking at all! I was lost and lonely and frightened and betrayed and you were there and...'

'And you thought you'd found a mug who would just step in and take care of you?'

'No! I never thought like that! I just couldn't! For one

thing, no one could ever take you for a mug and for another
I—'

Suddenly realising just what she had been about to let
fall, she clamped her mouth tight shut in panic, terrified
that she might have let a single syllable out. Had she really
been about to *say* it? Had she truly been so stupid as to
think she could risk telling him that she *loved him*? Her
stomach clenched painfully in horror at the thought.

'For another...?' Cesare echoed dangerously.

'For another, you weren't exactly bothered about that at
the time! All you seemed interested in was rushing me into
marriage so that you could get me into bed!'

That was the one comment that got through the red buzzing haze of fury in Cesare's mind. He couldn't deny it. He
wished he could, damn it, but the truth was that Megan had
hit the nail on the head. If he had been thinking straight,
he'd have asked her to have a proper check-up. He should
have taken her to the surgery himself, got everything
checked out.

But he hadn't been thinking straight. At least, he hadn't
been thinking with his *mind*, but with a far more basic part
of his anatomy. And that part hadn't wanted to wait around
to see if everything was exactly as he thought it. He'd been
quite happy to take Megan's word for it that she'd checked
everything out.

And now they were both trapped in this farce of a marriage. On the flowered cotton bedspread both his hands
clenched into tight, angry fists. Because he had let his feelings rule his head, because he had laid himself open to her
furious accusation—'All you seemed interested in was
rushing me into marriage so that you could get me into
bed.' And the way she had flung those words at him, the
expression on her face as she did so, made it plain just how
she felt about that!

In Megan's mind he was no better than Rowell had ever been. Seeing her as nothing but a body, one he had sexual designs on. And she had left him in no doubt that if she hadn't been desperate she would never have agreed to the wedding.

'You really think that?'

'You bet I do! I don't think—I *know*!' Megan flung back at him. 'Oh, come on! You're not going to try and deny it are you? Because if you did, quite frankly I wouldn't believe you.'

Her mouth spoke the words, but her mind told a different story.

Deny it, she pleaded. Please, please, deny it Cesare! Tell me that it was never that way! Tell me you married me for completely different reasons! Tell me you love me—or at least care for me—tell me anything at all and I'm so foolish, so weak that I'll believe every word you say.

But she had only to look into his face to know that there was no hope of her wish being granted. His expression had closed up, withdrawing totally from her, his jaw setting hard and his mouth just a thin, slash of a line. His eyes were like coal-black chips of ice, no emotion, no trace of warmth in them anywhere, and she anticipated his move even before he got to his feet.

'No,' he drawled cynically, his tone an insult in itself. 'I'm not going to deny it. I'd be a fool to even try when after all it's nothing but the truth. I wanted you in my bed, yes, and by asking you to marry me, I saw the perfect way to achieve that.'

She had been anticipating it, it was only what she had expected, so why did it hurt so much? Surely knowing already that that was all he wanted from her should have armoured her a little, protecting her vulnerable heart from the tearing pain of discovering that he was Gary Rowell all over again?

But somehow knowing that was what he was going to say only made it all the harder to take. It was like having her heart ripped out twice, giving her just long enough to experience the first pain as lethal before she experienced it once more, with new intensity this time.

'Well, thanks for telling me straight!' she returned with bleak flippancy. 'After all, I wouldn't want to labour under any delusions!'

Cesare's smile was grim, no trace of light reaching his eyes.

'Oh, I always speak the truth,' he snarled. 'Unlike some people.'

'I thought I was pregnant!'

'*Thought* isn't good enough!'

Cesare pushed himself upright, standing glowering down at her so ferociously that she shrank back against the pillows piled behind her.

'If you'd actually *thought* at all, *mia cara*, you would have done something more practical and not trapped both of us in this travesty of a marriage that we must regret for the rest of our days.'

'I—'

She had opened her mouth to declare that 'I will never regret it,' but looking into the cold, inimical depths of his eyes, she hastily bit back the words instead. He wouldn't believe them for one and seeing the mood he was in she was afraid to let him know the truth. It would make her too vulnerable, put her too much at risk where he was concerned.

'I couldn't agree more,' she quickly substituted instead.

'*Bene*. So now we both know where we stand. At least we agree on something.'

He was turning towards the door as he spoke. He had to get out of here now, he told himself. Had to leave before he opened his mouth really wide and said something he would always regret completely. The words were all there in his head, crowding into his thoughts so that he had to fight to hold them back and not let them come spilling out, betraying him for the fool he was.

Of course he hadn't thought to check whether she was truly pregnant. It hadn't even crossed his mind. All he had seen was the perfect opportunity to make Megan his and he had snatched at it without thinking. He hadn't even cared about love or the way she felt about him. She needed him and that was enough. He could fill that role until she decided she needed something more. And he had hoped that, given time, she might truly come to love him properly and they could turn their fake marriage into a real one for their own sakes, not just for the baby's.

But now it seemed that there was no baby after all. And without her back up against the wall, without the metaphorical gun pointing at her head, Megan had clearly realised just what a mistake she had made in marrying him. Every word she spoke revealed how much she regretted her impetuous action, and made it plain just how she felt at being trapped with him.

'What a pity you didn't start your period twenty-four hours earlier! That way you could have saved us both from a lot of heartache!'

'I was thinking exactly the same thing! That's something else we agree on!'

The irony was so dark, so savagely bitter that Cesare actually laughed out loud at it.

'*Now* we start to see eye to eye! What do you think, *cara*—perhaps if we stick at it, we might become soul mates in the end?'

'Never!'

Driven to the end of her control by the lash of his tongue, Megan couldn't control her own.

'I'd sooner spend the rest of my life in hell than have that happen! In fact, I'd prefer it if I never ever saw you again.'

'Your wish is my command...'

The sense of shock was like a blow to her head as she saw him sweep a low, mocking bow, the expression on his face turning the courtly gesture into something that was a million miles away from any politeness.

'That at least is something I can easily do for you.'

He meant it too, Megan realised shakenly as he turned on his heel again and marched to the door. She couldn't let him go! Not like this!

'But Cesare...' she croaked, not knowing if he had heard.

At first it seemed that, if he had, he was going to ignore her, but then, just in the doorway, he slowed, stilled.

'What?'

He didn't even turn; didn't look at her. He just tossed the question back over his shoulder without so much as a glance in her direction.

'The doctor said I could go home today. How am I going to get there?'

Cesare's breath hissed in between his teeth in a sound of barely-controlled fury and exasperation.

'I'll send the car for you,' he said at last. 'It'll be ready whenever you want it. Forgive me for not offering to come myself, but I truly believe that the less we see of each other right now, the better.'

CHAPTER EIGHT

'I TRULY believe that the less we see of each other right now, the better,' Cesare had said and he had meant it. If Megan had had any doubts that that was true, then they vanished very quickly in the days that followed her return home from the hospital.

The car and the chauffeur appeared to pick her up as he had promised, but of Cesare there was no sign, and he certainly didn't appear again in the house that night. Somehow he arranged for a housekeeper to move in on extremely short notice and be there in case she needed anything and to prepare meals, take care of the upkeep, but he never put in an appearance.

He stayed well away from the house until long after midnight when, worn out by the emotional upheaval of the day's events, she had finally crawled into bed. The sound of his car roaring up the drive and coming to a halt outside the door stirred her from the deep sleep of exhaustion into which she had collapsed, but she only had the energy to lift her head for a moment before dropping back onto the pillow with a sigh of despair and drifting away again.

He was gone again before she woke up in the morning. And he had slept somewhere else in the house. The other side of the big bed was unrumpled and undisturbed by the lean muscular frame of the man who was her husband in law, if not in reality. There was no trace of the scent of Cesare's skin, no imprint of his head on the pillow, no lingering warmth of his body on the sheets. He might not have existed for all the evidence he left behind.

And that was how life was for the next week. Day after day Megan tried desperately to catch a glimpse of the man she had married, and failed. She sat up late at night, only to find that he had stayed out so long that she fell asleep before he returned. Or she woke up early in the morning, determined to catch him before he left. But it seemed that he had some sort of sixth sense where she was concerned and on the one day she was sure that no one could have got up and out before her, it turned out that he had stayed in town, booking into an hotel instead.

It was ten days before she saw him again. And then that was only because she totally refused to give in this time. She turned all the downstairs lights off so that it looked as if there was no one in the house then seated herself in the most uncomfortable chair in the sitting room, where there was no chance at all of her dropping off to sleep. Positioning the chair by the doorway, looking out into the main hall so that she would know immediately if the front door opened, she settled herself—and waited.

And waited.

In the end she nearly missed him. In spite of her discomfort, the lateness of the hour almost caught up with her. Her eyes began to close, and it was only the sound of a key in the lock that stirred her from her doze and, blinking hard, she watched the big, carved oak door swing open.

He was dressed for the office, in one of the sleekly tailored, elegant business suits he always wore to work. His shirt was fine white linen, slightly crumpled after the heat of the early-August day, and his understated maroon and blue tie had been tugged unfastened and hung loose around his neck, giving him the slightly dissolute look of someone returning home from a late-night party.

Megan's heart kicked hard at just the sight of him. It seemed as if, in the short time since she had seen him, her need for him had grown stronger, her appetite for his appeal sharpening with each day's deprivation until she was hungry for his presence. Never before had the appeal of darkly tanned skin against the crisp whiteness of his shirt, the long, lean lines of his body, the strong chest tapering to a narrow waist and then moving down into the power of seemingly endless legs, come home to her with quite so much force. The sensual impact of his appearance took her breath away and deprived her totally of the ability to speak.

And in the same moment Cesare caught sight of her sitting in the doorway. He stood stock-still, glanced behind him for a second as if considering the chances of escape back into the night, then obviously decided against it. Shutting the door with what seemed to Megan to be totally unnecessary and excessive precision, he shrugged himself out of his jacket, hooked one finger into the collar and tossed the coat casually over his shoulder. Strolling forward with an apparently casual and relaxed attitude, he came to a halt a couple of feet away from her and looked straight into her wary face.

'Good evening, Megan. And to what do I owe the pleasure of your presence here tonight?'

Privately Megan took the liberty of doubting that it was any sort of a pleasure, and she suspected that the question, as well as the tone in which it had been delivered, was meant to put her mentally off balance. It very nearly succeeded, and she had a nasty little fight with herself in order to hold her ground and not actually give in to an impulse to run from the obviously hostile expression in his dark eyes.

'Do you know the phrase about Mohammed and the mountain?' she managed unevenly.

'I believe I've heard of it. Something about if Mohammed won't come to the mountain…'

'Then the mountain must come to Mohammed.'

'And in this case, am I to understand that you are taking on the role of the mountain? Really, Megan, you do yourself a great disservice. No man alive could ever describe you as being at all mountain-like. As a matter of fact, I think that you appear to have lost some weight since I last saw you.'

Megan didn't doubt it. Her appetite had totally deserted her over the past week and the housekeeper had been openly disapproving of the way the tempting meals she served every day had been sent away virtually untouched, barely a few mouthfuls actually consumed. And when Megan had put on the mustard-coloured cotton dress tonight she had been painfully aware of the way that the waist hung loose on her, the V-neck gaping at the front.

'If that's meant to distract me, then I'm afraid it won't work. If anything, it simply emphasises just how long it is since we've actually seen each other.'

'I've been busy.'

'During your *honeymoon*? I doubt if that's the way most newly-married husbands carry on.'

'But then I'm not exactly a traditional newly-married husband, am I?' Cesare shot back cynically. 'And I hardly think that anyone would describe this as a conventional sort of a marriage.'

'Perhaps not,' Megan had to concede. 'But you were the one who insisted that people should believe that we did have a proper marriage. That in public at least we should give the impression that we're truly husband and wife. We're hardly going to do that if you're never here and I'm on my own all day.'

'So now I'm neglecting you!' Cesare drawled satirically. '*Perdone me, cara*, I thought you never wanted to see me again. I did not know that you had changed your mind.'

'You know perfectly well that what I said was an exaggeration! Just as you know we can't go on like this. Cesare, we have to talk!'

'Have to?' he echoed dangerously, making her nerves twist themselves into tight, painful knots of apprehension and fear.

But then, just when she had convinced herself that he was not prepared to listen to a word she said; that he was about to turn right round and walk out of the house again, not even sparing her a backward glance, he lifted his broad shoulders in a dismissive shrug and spread his hands in a very Italian gesture of surrender.

'D'accordo, innamorata! If you wish to talk then we will talk.'

He strolled into the room sliding past her chair with elegant care so that in spite of the narrow and constricting space he avoided all contact with her by the merest inch.

Crossing to the drinks cabinet, he pulled out a bottle of red wine, splashed a lavish amount of it into a glass, and sipped appreciatively.

'So talk! Oh, *scusi…*'

His apology was a deliberate and overelaborate afterthought.

'Did you want a drink, darling?'

Knowing she was being deliberately provoked, Megan could only shake her head silently. It was either that or explode completely, ruining any possible chance she had of holding any sort of reasonable discussion with him.

'No thanks.'

Realising the way he had put her at a disadvantage if she remained where she was, needing to twist her head awkwardly on her neck in order to be able to see him, she got up and walked over to the soft leather chesterfield set into the wide bay window of the room. Sinking down onto it, she curled her legs up underneath and settled in for what she suspected was going to be a very hard and very long night.

'Are you sure? You seem on edge—it might relax you. And as we both know, you don't have to worry about your alcohol intake any more. There's no one else you can harm if you have a drink.'

'I'm fine without a drink, thanks.'

She wanted to keep a clear head. Cesare in this mood was dangerous and she didn't dare risk provoking him any more than she could help.

'And if that nasty dig about my being able to drink now was meant to point out to me the stupid mistake I made in believing I was pregnant, then let me assure you I don't need any reminding of that fact. I've thought about it all week—in fact, I've hardly thought about anything else. And I've made up my mind just what we have to do.'

'You have?'

Cesare had lifted his glass to his lips, had been about to take a sip of his wine, but now he lowered it again slowly, looking at her across the top. The suspicion in the sharply narrowed brown eyes was like a brutal knife in Megan's already vulnerable heart. Did he really hate her so much that he didn't trust a word she said?

'And what conclusion have you come to?'

He moved to take a seat opposite her, leaning back in the big armchair with an apparent ease and nonchalance that did nothing to disguise the way he was watching her, the cold, assessing stare that was fixed on her face. Megan felt dangerously exposed and vulnerable, unable to meet the burning force of his scrutiny head-on.

'One I think you'll approve of.'

She had looked at the problem from every possible angle all through the long, lonely hours when he was avoiding her, and had come up with the only possible answer she could think of. It would be so very, very hard. It would break her heart, but it was the one thing she could do for him. If he didn't want her love then at least she could give him his freedom. Biting her lip to regain control and force back the weak tears that threatened, she forced herself to continue.

'Oh, don't look so worried Cesare. What I plan to do is to set you free. It's quite simple really—it's the obvious answer.'

'Is there an obvious answer?'

'I think so.'

'Enlighten me.'

'This marriage was a mistake from the start—and it's even more so now. But we don't have to stay together. It'll be so easy to separate. And as we never actually—never...'

'Consummated the relationship,' he finished for her with an understanding that was blatantly insincere.

'Well, yes...so we don't even need a divorce. We can just get an annulment.'

'*No!*'

'No?'

Megan couldn't understand it. Wasn't this what he wanted? She had felt so sure he would appreciate the chance to get free of her.

'No!'

Cesare flung himself to his feet, his eyes cold, his jaw tight with rejection. Even his nostrils flared in disgust and disapproval. He was pure, unreformed, Sicilian male from the top of his silky dark hair to the soles of his handmade leather boots.

'You think that I would let you do that? That I would let you go—just walk out on our marriage—not even a fortnight after our wedding night, for God's sake! It isn't going to happen. I won't let you!'

It was the roar of a wounded lion, and he knew it. Deep inside, he admitted to himself that if she was determined to go, if she didn't want to stay, then nothing he could do would keep her there. And the appalling thing was the way that, in spite of everything, he still wanted to keep her.

He had been furious at first; blinded by the blazing anger that had possessed him when he had learned that she wasn't actually pregnant. At that moment he had been the one who had thought of walking out on their marriage, ending it right then and there. He had forced himself to go into work, running the gauntlet of joking, disbelieving comments from his staff who had known that he had just got married and couldn't believe he wasn't with his wife, in order to give himself time. Time to think, to calm down and look at what had happened objectively. To try and decide just what he wanted out of this relationship now.

And the one thing that he had kept coming back to was that he still wanted Megan. He didn't care how much she wanted out of the marriage; he wasn't going to let her go without a fight. And if that meant fighting her as well, then that was how it had to be. All he wanted was to win a little time. Time to try and redeem something from this nightmare of a marriage into which they'd fallen.

And to be perfectly honest, he didn't really give a damn how he went about it.

'You are not walking away from me, or this marriage. What the hell do you imagine people will think?'

'I don't care what people will think.'

'Well I do! You'd destroy any pride I have amongst my family, my people. I'd be a man who couldn't even keep his wife by his side for a month or more! A man who, if you ask for an annulment, apparently cannot even *make love* to his wife.'

'Oh…I hadn't looked at it that way. But what else can we do? There's no other alternative.'

'There is one. We stay married.'

'No…'

Her shudder revealed how much the idea horrified her. 'We *can't*!'

'We can,' he contradicted flatly. 'And we will. Oh, Megan, *cara*, don't look so horrified. I promise you it won't be as bad as you think.'

She watched him warily as he prowled nearer, not coming close enough to touch, but near enough to set all her senses fizzing, to put the scent of him into her nostrils, to make her want to reach out, feel that bronzed skin under her fingertips. But that was a weakness she couldn't give in to and so she folded her hands tightly in her lap and clenched her fingers hard.

'But things will have to change.'

Cesare made it sound as if he was thinking things through, as if each new idea was just occurring to him, but every instinct told Megan that that was just not the case. For one thing, Cesare Santorino never spoke without thinking, and for another there was a light in his eyes that warned of a cool, astute brain working very very calmly and very very confidently towards an end it had already decided on. An end that he had every intention of achieving.

'This marriage we have is no marriage at all. No Sicilian would put up with a marriage in name only. No Sicilian would let it even be *thought* that he had never made love to his wife.'

'No…' Megan put in, seeing only too well just where this was leading, and trying desperately to deflect him from his purpose. But the only thing her interjection achieved was a faint pause, a sudden stillness in which deep brown eyes locked with uncertain green, and then Cesare's low, beautifully accented voice began again.

'No?' he questioned, softly, hypnotically, effortlessly weaving a sensual spell around her already tangled thoughts. 'That is not what you said in the library less than a month ago, *cara*. Nor again in the wedding service when you vowed to—'

'They're just words!' Megan snapped, getting to her feet in a rush.

Although he was still carefully keeping his distance she felt far too vulnerable sitting down, having to crane her neck up to look into his beautiful face. She needed to look at him head-on, though as soon as she did her nerves tangled painfully as she saw the brilliant glitter of implacable resolution burning in his eyes.

'Words you said in a church,' he reminded her with malign softness. 'Words you swore would be true until death do us part.'

'I...'

It was no good! Looking into his face deprived her of the power of speech. And so she dragged her eyes away from the stunning features, forced them instead onto the strong, tanned hands that rested on the back of a chair.

And this was no better. If anything, it was far, far worse! All she could think of was the way those hands had touched her, the caresses they had delivered, the pleasure they had given her. Just to look at them made her feel as if the blunt tips of the long fingers were actually wandering across her skin, making her shiver in sheer delight, wanting to purr like a cat that has been stroked into a delirium of pleasure.

'Be my guest...'

She blinked in confusion and astonishment as Cesare

moved suddenly, lifting one arm and holding it out to her so that all she would have to do would be to raise her own hand and she would come into contact with him.

'What…?'

'Don't hold back. I won't mind…'

His smile, enticed, drew her in, as he unfastened the cuff of the shirt, pushing back the white sleeve all the way to the elbow. Then he held out his arm again, closer this time. So close that she had only to breathe in and she could smell the clean, faintly musky scent of his skin.

'Touch me, Megan,' Cesare urged. 'I know you want to. I've seen it in your eyes.'

'No you haven't!'

To her horror her fingers actually twitched convulsively at her sides, fighting against the restraint she was imposing on them and she had to forcibly hold them still. But Cesare had seen the movement and his smile deepened.

'You lie very badly, you know.'

'I'm not lying!'

'In the same way that you're not tempted, hmm? Okay, *amante*, let's see how strong your resolve truly is.'

And to Megan's total consternation he moved his hand away from her and on to the tie still loosely hanging around his neck. With an arrogant little flick of his wrist he pulled the tie free, tossed it to one side, heedless of where it landed, his eyes holding hers. Then he moved on to the white pearlised buttons of his shirt.

She couldn't tear her eyes away, could only watch, transfixed, as he slid first one and then the next free of their fastenings, the actions opening the neck of the fine shirt, exposing the strong lines of his throat, the smooth lines of his throat, the smooth skin of his shoulders, the point where a pulse beat steadily and strongly.

His chest was almost as tanned as his arms; rich bronze

satin hazed with black curling hair. And as yet more buttons slid open she was intensely, heatedly aware of the way that the line of hair traced a tantalising path down towards his waist, disappearing tormentingly below the fine leather belt that encircled his narrow waist.

Just how far would he go? She wondered as the last button was undone and the shirt, tugged free at his waist, fell fully open. If she didn't stop him, would he perform a complete striptease right here in front of her? Would he shrug off the shirt as he had his jacket on his arrival home? And what would follow then? The trousers? More? Her throat tightened and dried just to think of it.

'Touch me...' Cesare urged again, his voice dropping a husky octave lower.

Somehow Megan forced herself to shake her head again and heard his low, dark laughter.

'A coward as well as a liar. Okay...'

She didn't know if he really meant to close up his shirt again or not. Simply the threat of it was enough to drive her into action. She couldn't stand there silent any longer.

'Wait!'

The word was torn from her, impossible to hold back, and in almost the same instant her hand went out, fingers splayed, reaching for that tempting expanse of dark skin.

Cesare stilled instantly, silent, waiting.

There was no way she could stop herself. It was as inevitable as breathing, as the way one heartbeat followed another.

No turning back. The words sounded in her mind as her fingertips made burning contact with the hard wall of his chest and she knew that she was lost.

CHAPTER NINE

His flesh felt like heated satin, smooth and soft under her touch. But beneath that again were the hard lines of bone and sinew, the play of powerful muscles as they bunched and flexed under the tips of her fingers. In the moment that she'd touched him, he'd frozen, standing immobile, scarcely breathing, as she let her fingers wander over his exposed chest.

And it was that very stillness, when combined with his total silence, that gave her the courage to indulge herself, explore the strong masculine contours of his torso as she wanted. If he had so much as moved an inch, or said a single word, then she would have panicked like a nervous bird startled by a cat, spreading its wings in instant flight.

But Cesare sensed intuitively that movement and speech would spoil the moment, shatter the delicate mood in an instant, and he stayed motionless under her touch, though the bitter-chocolate eyes watched her every move, following the path of her caressing fingers over his body, studying her absorbed face as she discovered everything about him.

Each new spot held a fascinating discovery, from the curling crispness of the black hair, the curving framework of his ribcage, to the dark, tight nubs of his male nipples that hardened instantly under her touch. This time he could not hold back the swiftly indrawn breath that was his instinctive response to the caress and the faint sound brought her eyes instantly to his, so that he saw how her pupils had enlarged and darkened, leaving only the faintest rim of green at the outer edge.

'Megan…' he began, but immediately swallowed down the rest of his words, fearful that he might have broken the trance that held her, destroyed the beginnings of the trust that had built up between them.

But then Megan smiled and again he caught his breath, but this time in delight. The blend of shyness and uncertainty, combined with a subtle but undeniable provocation, a hint of teasing seduction was irresistible, heating the blood in his veins until its warmth flooded his body in the space of a heartbeat.

'Megan…' he tried again, angling his head so that he could capture her mouth, needing to touch her, to kiss her, or he would explode.

But she slipped away from him, dodging his caress with a smiling ease, one soft hand coming up to lie across his lips, hold back the kiss he had tried to give her. So instead he pressed the caress on her fingers, loving the feel of her, the taste of her skin. Slowly, delicately he moved his mouth up and along each one, kissing each inch of skin he encountered, and he heard her sigh of response, felt the warmth of her breath against his lips, soft as the brush of a butterfly's wings.

When her hands closed over the edges of his shirt, slipping the fine linen back and over his shoulders, down the taut lines of his arms, he felt his heart pick up pace in immediate response, thudding heavily inside his chest, making his blood pound round his body. His hunger for her was already an ache that was close to pain, the swollen shaft of his desire straining at the confines of his clothes, depriving him of the ability to think of anything but the way that he needed her.

'*Cara*,' he groaned, knowing he would soon be unable to take any more. '*Amante.*'

His shirt had gone, removed from his back and dropped

carelessly on the floor, but there was no time to feel the chill of the night air against his skin. Instead, his clothing was replaced by the warm touch of Megan's hands, the soft pressure of her lips, the moist trail of her tongue that was almost more than he could bear.

'Do you know what you are doing to me?'

Once more there was that slanting, upward glance, and this time there was no smile in her eyes, only a dark intensity of need that matched his own.

'I think so,' she murmured.

'Then let me make sure…'

At last he allowed himself to move, his hands coming out, closing over her arms, grabbing her and dragging her close. Her head was tilted back, her mouth so close, inviting his kiss.

And he took that invitation; took her mouth with all the force of the need that had come close to driving him insane. He had thought that the kiss might ease some of the pressure, that the deep, demanding power of the caress might appease some of the hunger, give him a chance to draw breath, slow the pace, consider her needs as well as his own.

It had the opposite effect.

From the moment that their lips met, he was lost. Hot waves of desire were breaking over his head and he was going down rapidly, drowning in the sensual currents that were tugging at all his senses, dragging him under, making him lose himself in the surf.

'*This* is what you do to me…' he muttered against her yielding mouth, snatching wild, almost angry kisses and returning them one thousandfold to her lips. '*This* is how you make me feel!'

She didn't need the words, Megan thought hazily. No speech could communicate anything of the urgency, the passion, more clearly than his touch, his kisses, the heat of his burningly aroused body crushed against hers. Words were too cool, too rational, too *controlled*. And she wanted nothing of control, nothing of restraint. She wanted only fire and heat and thunder crashing in the darkness while lightning split the sky with its brilliance.

'Show me...' she formed the words raggedly, gasping them out between the wild, erotic kisses he showered upon her willing mouth. 'Show me...'

His response was the rough sound of laughter deep in his throat.

'Oh, I'll show you, *cara*. I'll show you how you make me feel—how much I want you. I'll show you how I make love to my wife—how I stamp my imprint on you, drive you to an ecstasy so wild, so hot, that you'll never recover. Never be able to look at another man again.'

'I don't want any other man...'

Megan's voice was raw round the edges. Her mind felt as if it was coming apart, unravelling and fraying in the force of the wild tempest of desire that swirled around her, trapping her in its primitive power.

'No other man but you...only you.'

They were the last coherent words she could manage, because the next moment, with his mouth still hard on hers, his hands had come between them wrenching open the buttons on the cotton dress, and pulling it open. Haste made his fingers clumsy, breaking one of the buttons off and sending it spinning away across the floor to land with a faint rattle against the skirting board under the window.

Neither of them even saw it go. They were too intent on each other, too busy touching, smoothing, kissing. Megan's fingers closed over the wide strength of Cesare's shoulders, clutching tight and digging deep into the hard muscles of his back. Her breath caught in her throat as she felt the heat of his fingers against the undersides of her breasts, the way they sought and found the front fastening to her bra and dispensed with it swiftly and easily. As the soft weight fell free into his waiting palms, her body arched towards him, her head flung back, offering the lush curves his fingers had exposed to the burning caress of his mouth.

A high, abandoned, crooning sound broke from her as she felt his tongue touch her straining nipple, draw a flaming circle round the aching peak then move to treat the other breast to the same tormenting delight. She was lost, adrift on a tidal wave of excitement, the throbbing pulse between her legs burning white-hot, making her crush her yearning body against his, sliding the cradle of her hips up and down and over the force of his erection.

'Megan!'

Her name was like a foreign sound on his lips. She hardly recognised him, hardly knew herself in this wild, wanton woman whose frantic hands clutched in the black silk of his hair, whose lips were swollen from his kisses, her dress half on half hanging gaping from her shoulders.

She didn't even pause to think or to object when Cesare ripped the rest of the buttons apart, not pausing even to attempt to open them properly. The next moment he had wrenched the dress down the slim length of her body, abandoning it in a crumpled heap on the carpet as he lifted her high off the floor. Acting purely instinctively, she wrapped her slender legs around his waist, squeezing tight as she bent her head and plundered his mouth as fiercely as he had taken hers.

She knew that he was moving but she didn't know where. Had no sense of anything beyond Cesare until he tumbled her down onto the settee, coming down hard on top of her, pressing her into the burgundy velvet cushions, imprisoning her with the weight of his body. And somehow in the flurry of movement, the scrap of ice-blue silk and lace that was all her remaining clothing had been taken from her too, leaving the last, most heated, most intimate part of her exposed to his predatory hands.

And Cesare took full advantage of the fact. The long powerful fingers probed and caressed, awakening, tantalising, arousing, driving her to distraction. He took her to the edge of a precipice, held her there, and then, just when she was sure she must take flight and tumble headlong, he brought her back, kept her waiting yet.

Again and again he did it, tormenting her with almost, with not yet, with *wait*, until she was writhing desperately under him, covering his face with frantic kisses and whispering urgently in her ear. Pleading with him to take pity on her, have mercy, release her from this most sensuous of torments. And it was only when she was totally beside herself with need that he parted her legs with a non-too gentle nudge from a powerful thigh, slid between them, and buried himself in her aching, yearning body.

It was all she needed. Her eyes opened wide in one brief moment of shocked delight, her whole body stiffened, arced, then seemed to explode from deep within, her mind splintering into a shower of golden stars that swept all awareness from her other than the deepest, wildest, most glorious sensation she had ever known.

And Cesare was not long behind her. From the moment that he had felt the intimate warmth of her inner muscles close about him he was lost, incapable of any control. It was hard and fast and hot and strong, and so fierce that his head went back and a wild, primitive cry broke from his throat as he too reached his climax and collapsed, his big chest heaving, on top of her again.

It was the start of a night like none Megan had ever known. A night in which she discovered sensations she had never known existed. Found pleasure spots on her body, and in her mind, that she had never suspected had ever been there before. She learned how to please Cesare and he in turn taught her how every inch of her flesh responded to his slightest touch by coming wildly awake, passionately demanding and taking everything he had to give. And in the process she unearthed a whole new part of herself, a different, grown-up woman, with a woman's needs, a woman's pleasures. A woman that no one had ever uncovered before; the woman that only Cesare could show her she really was.

She supposed that at some point they must have slept, if only for a moment or two. But if she did, she was not aware of it, except as a time of recovery, a space in which she drew breath, recouped her strength and recovered from one wild sexual onslaught enough to be hungry enough to submit to another. And, in those brief spaces of time, Cesare must have taken her up in his arms and carried her to the other parts of the house she found herself in when her consciousness slowly returned to her again.

The first time she came back to herself in the bathroom where he took her into the shower and gently washed the sweat from her body with tender, almost reverential hands. But, in the space of a couple of stirring heartbeats, that touch changed from gentle to demanding from demanding to arousing and once more their passion overtook them, hot and strong as the water that pounded down on their heads, sluiced their shuddering bodies. Megan could only be thankful that Cesare had the strength to carry her from the steamy cubicle and wrap her in a thick white towel before dropping down on the bed beside her, his heart still thudding, his breathing uneven.

'This is what I wanted from you,' he managed, reaching out and pulling her close, folding his arms round her and tucking her up against the hard strength of his body. 'Why I married you. Why you can only ever be mine.'

By the time the slow pink fingers of the early dawn began to creep over the horizon flooding the bedroom with the first early threads of light, while outside the waking birds began to sing their loud, joyful chorus to the dawn, Megan had lost count of how many times they had actually made love.

She only knew that every limb and muscle ached with exhaustion, so that she had to bite back a groan of weariness when she moved, and her eyelids were too heavy to open even halfway. But she had never been happier or more fulfilled in her life. Her whole body was sated with pleasure, filled and totally content, in a way she had never ever known before.

Sighing happily to herself, she wriggled nearer to Cesare's long, relaxed body, curving against him so that her back fitted along his front, the curves of her buttocks pressed into the cradle of his pelvis. In his sleep he stirred faintly, expelled a low, weary sigh, and then his arms came out, enclosing her tightly and holding her close again.

This was a new beginning, Megan told herself. A new beginning in the dawn of a new day. No matter how badly things had gone wrong before, surely now they could start all over again, this time as husband and wife, and learn how to have a proper marriage. Surely now, after a night like this, they had a hope of getting it right.

Because if there was one thing tonight had taught her it was that Cesare was the one, the only man for her. She had always known it, even as an adolescent, but then she had loved him in an immature way, with the love of a child, a teenager in the throes of her first crush. As a result, she had lost her way for a brief, foolish moment and so she had fallen out of love with him—or thought she had—stupidly, naïvely falling in to Gary's arms in the bitter pain of rejection on the rebound.

But Gary had never made her feel like this. He had never even come close. Compared with this, Gary's selfish, inconsiderate taking of her body paled as strongly as the flickering light of a candle was reduced to nothing in the full force of the glow of the sun. What she had known with him could never have been called lovemaking, never had come within light-years of being anything remotely like the sort of ecstasy that Cesare had shown her not just once but each and every time he had possessed her body.

And, just as she was sure that she could never feel this with anyone else, she was convinced at some deepest, most instinctual level of thought, that Cesare could never have made love to her as he had without feeling something similar for her. Perhaps he wouldn't yet call it love. Maybe he didn't even recognise it as that right now—but it was there, and given time and nurturing it could only develop, grow stronger, until it took possession of his soul as it had of hers.

And when that time came then she knew that he would finally admit the truth. That he would finally recognise what was in his heart and tell her that he loved her.

And, with the prospect of more nights like this ahead of her, with more physical expressions of his love to keep her going until her husband could bring himself to say the word, she knew she would have the strength to wait. She could even let him take his time. Deep in her soul, she knew that the moment would be worth it when it finally arrived.

And so, with her body fulfilled and satisfied, her mind a glow of happy anticipation, and a smile of pure happiness softly curving her lips, she nestled even closer to the man she adored and drifted deeply asleep.

It was many, many hours later when she finally struggled back to the surface of consciousness, forcing open sleep-sealed lids to the brilliance of a mid-morning sun that made her wince and fling her arm up to protect her eyes.

'So you're awake at last.'

It was Cesare's voice, low and husky. The most wonderful, most welcome sound in all the world.

'I thought you were going to sleep the day away.'

'And if I had done, then whose fault would that be?'

Peering through her fingers, she squinted up at his dark, handsome face, silhouetted against the fine voile curtains at the windows.

'You wore me out last night—drained me of all the energy I possessed.'

'And how do you feel now?'

'Wonderful,' Megan assured him, stretching luxuriously. 'Absolutely wonderful. In fact, I'd like to stay feeling that way all day long. So why don't you come back into bed?'

His silence was unexpected. Shockingly so. It had her opening her eyes wide and looking into his face in a rush of concern.

'Cesare?'

'Can't be done.'

The answer came smoothly enough, but not quite quickly enough to erase the sudden feeling of chilling unease that crept over her skin, draining the blissful warmth from it.

'You need to get up and get dressed. We have a plane waiting for us at the airport.'

'We do? Where are we going?'

'To Sicily. Remember that honeymoon we were supposed to have—well, we're starting it now. My parents want to meet you and I want to show you my country. After all you're a Sicilian's wife now. It's time you got to know the island.'

'A Sicilian's wife,' Megan echoed, not quite sure how to take the words.

'My wife,' she would have understood of course. It would have meant so much to hear herself described that way. But 'a Sicilian's wife' had a very different sort of sound to it, one that was harshly possessive and yet impersonal, with strands of something ominous running through it, dark notes that she couldn't even begin to interpret. It came uncomfortably close to the arrogant declaration Cesare had made the night before, just before he had performed that amazing striptease that had led to them making love for the first time.

Things would have to change, he had declared. 'No Sicilian would put up with a marriage in name only. No Sicilian would let it even be *thought* that he had never made love to his wife.'

In spite of the heat of the day and the soft, summer-weight quilt covering her, Megan suddenly felt her blood run icy in her veins, chilling her whole body. While she had lain here last night, lost in the happy delusion that Cesare could not have made love to her as he had without some deeper, more emotional feeling than just plain sex, had he in fact been thinking—and feeling—something else entirely?

'So—we're staying married?' she ventured uncertainly.

'Of course we're staying married!' Cesare declared, arrogantly dismissing any doubts she might have had. Doubts he clearly didn't even recognise could possibly exist. 'Surely after last night you've forgotten all that nonsense about separating? Because if you haven't, it's about time you did. One thing's for sure, *cara*, you certainly won't have a hope in hell of asking for an annulment.'

CHAPTER TEN

'I've fallen in love with your island—with Sicily...' Megan told Cesare. 'And with your family.'

Her husband stirred slightly on the hot sand of the tiny bay and looked up at her through eyes narrowed against the glare of the sun.

'And they have fallen in love with you,' he murmured lazily. 'So much so that they've forgiven us for having a rushed, almost secret, English wedding instead of the traditional big family event here on the island. Mama always expected that she would get to invite all her friends and their families when I married.'

'She's still managed to do that, all the same.'

Megan smiled, thinking of the huge party Isabella Santorino had held in their honour during their first week on the island. It had been incredible, with huge trestle tables laid out under the fig trees in the open air, covered in starched white linen cloths and piled high with food. It had seemed as if every member of the Sicilian community from Palermo to Siracusa had converged on the huge old, white-painted farmhouse to celebrate that day.

'Each time I thought that surely everyone was here, someone else turned up—another uncle, or a cousin.'

'Oh, we couldn't miss anyone out, right down to the second cousins six times removed.' Cesare grinned. 'We would never hear the end of it if we did. It's the only way we can make up for not doing things properly according to tradition.'

'A big white wedding?'

'Huge.'

Cesare manoeuvred himself upright and sat, arms wrapped round his knees, staring out at the softly lapping, deep-blue sea.

'With all the formalities observed. The engagement shouldn't even have been announced until our parents had met and been formally introduced *in casa*. In my mother's eyes, what we did was only a little more embarrassing than if we had indulged in the *fuitina*.'

'*Fuitina*...' Megan echoed curiously. 'What's that?'

'It means lovers' flight.'

Cesare scooped up a fistful of sand then opened his fingers and watched as it slowly trickled away, back onto the beach.

'It's part of Sicilian history, but it's still a reality in some parts of the island today. If a young couple—teenagers—fell in love but they couldn't sleep together, then they ran away instead. Their flight showed their serious intentions to their family, and they would be given a room in a relative's house in which to consummate their "marriage". When they were older and self-supporting then their union would be legalised.'

'That's surprisingly liberated,' Megan commented. Even her short time on the island had taught her that young Sicilian women in particular were subject to parental controls that she and her friends would have considered downright archaic.

'It's pragmatic,' Cesare contradicted. 'It was also a way of saving the girl's honour. If she were to sleep with her boyfriend without family sanction, she would be considered as little better than a *puttana*—a prostitute.'

'Has it ever happened in your family?'

'No—though I remember that Gio threatened to run away with Lucia if their respective parents didn't sanction their marriage. They were both only sixteen when they met, and he never looked at anyone else after that.'

'He must have loved her very much.'

'She was his life; his whole reason for existing. That's why it hit him so very badly when she died.'

'I'm not surprised.'

In spite of the heat of the day, Megan shivered and goosebumps pricked at the skin of her arms exposed by the sleeveless, V-necked sundress she wore in much the same sort of deep-turquoise colour as the sunlit sea out in the bay.

'It must be terrible to lose someone you love so very much, and so young too.'

Lucia Cardella had been barely thirty when she had died. Just the same age as Cesare now. Megan didn't know how she could bear to live if she lost her husband as Gio had lost his wife.

'At least Gio has started to come back to life since you arrived. You've helped him see that life does go on.'

'Time has done that for him,' Megan chose her words carefully. 'He can't mourn his wife for ever, no matter how much he loved her.'

'But you and he have got on so very well together. It's clear he can talk to you about Lucia and how much he misses her.'

Was he jealous? Megan wondered. Was there even the faintest touch of annoyance or disapproval in his tone? She would have welcomed it. Would have welcomed any trace of any emotion that would give her some indication of just how this husband of hers felt about her.

They had been in Sicily for four weeks now. Four weeks in which the pretence of a honeymoon, the pretence of having a real marriage, had been played out under the burning Italian sun. She knew that Cesare's parents were deceived.

That every friend or business acquaintance they saw believed that she was truly Signora Santorino, in the fullest sense of the title. No one even suspected that their marriage was not the whirlwind love-match they claimed it to be, their wedding as much the impulsive action of two people who couldn't bear to be apart as the *fuitina* Cesare had just described to her.

But Gio had been different. Perhaps because he had known a true, deep, once in a lifetime sort of love with Lucia, he had recognised the same when he saw it in Megan's eyes. He had known from the start the way she felt about his half-brother and, unlike anyone else, he had also guessed at something of the unhappiness and emptiness deep at the centre of their relationship.

So she could talk to Gio in a way she couldn't talk to his half-brother. And because Gio was so similar to Cesare with his jet-black hair and ebony-dark eyes, she sometimes allowed herself to dream that she was in fact talking to her husband in a way that her fears would never allow her to.

Which was why she would have welcomed any show of jealousy. She wouldn't even have cared if Cesare had become angry at her relationship with his brother. Because at least it would have shown that he cared.

'I like Gio,' she said now. 'I wish he could find someone to make his life whole again.'

'I don't think that's possible. Lucia was the one for him, and I doubt if he will ever find anyone to replace her.'

'But Paolo needs a mother.'

Cesare had got to his feet and was brushing the sand off his jeans, his dark head bent and the strands of the gleaming black hair falling forward over his face as he concentrated on the simple task.

'Paolo has his father. And Gio won't marry just any woman purely to provide his son with a mother. The men in our family fall heavily when they fall in love. It's been that way for generations, my father knew in the moment he first saw her that Mama was the one for him, even if she was married to Gio's father at the time. And his father was the same before that.'

'But Gio's a Cardella…'

'It works for his side of the family too.'

He straightened up, brown eyes clashing with green for a second.

'For all of us.'

All of us. He was talking about himself as well. Telling her that he too had known the moment he had set eyes on the woman he wanted, that she was the one for him. That like his father and grandfather he had known that blinding flash of sensation that had told him this was the love of his life.

From the back of her mind came the memory of the day in the library, the day he had asked her to marry him.

'Like you, I fell in love with the wrong person,' he had said. 'Years ago. I was little more than a child. Same age as you if you must know.'

And clearly that unknown woman, whoever she was, had not returned his feelings. Perhaps she had spurned his love, married someone else.

Suddenly it was as if the sun had gone behind a cloud, taking all the warmth out of the day and destroying the more relaxed, easy mood they had shared earlier.

It was no wonder that Cesare didn't care how long she spent talking to his brother. Hardly surprising that the show of any emotion that she hoped for never came. He didn't love her, didn't care *enough* for it to matter. His heart had been given to someone else, long ago and, like Gio, there would never be anyone to replace her.

That was why he had been able to propose marriage in

the coolly indifferent, businesslike way he had done when he had believed she was pregnant. He couldn't have the woman he wanted, but she would do as a substitute. A second-rate substitute, she told herself, wincing at the way the thought twisted a cruel knife in her already desolated heart. He *wanted* her; he desired her sexually. But his love she would never have.

'It's time we were heading back...'

Cesare held out a hand to help her up from the soft sand. 'Are you ready?'

No, Megan wanted to say. No, she wasn't ready to leave. She didn't want to go home at all. She had loved every moment of the time they had spent in this beautiful little cove just around the coast from the busy, sophisticated and tourist-crowded beaches of Mondello and overlooked by the high slopes of Mount Pellegrino.

They had brought a picnic with them and, after they had swum in the warm blue sea, they had eaten it lazily lying on the soft sand, chatting desultorily, talking about nothing important. But even that had been magical to Megan because Cesare had admitted that this was a special place to him. He had wanted to show her one of his favourite spots from when he had been a boy.

'Megan?'

'Oh, yes, I suppose so.'

She wished she didn't have to take his hand, but it would look too pointed if she didn't. It would make him angry, and these days she would do anything to avoid making him angry. She could cope with life as long as it jogged along at the pace they'd kept to since they'd arrived in Sicily. On the island, Cesare was a different man; more relaxed, mellower, easier to get along with—as long a she didn't do anything to rock the boat. And she was determined not to rock the boat.

Each day that they managed to keep the peace between them was one more that went into building up some sense of a real relationship together. Like bricks in a wall, the hours combined, creating a foundation on which she hoped—prayed—they could establish a stable marriage, one that maybe, just maybe, would turn into the proper thing.

If they could talk, spend time together, relax together as they had done on this beach today then slowly she might come to mean more to him than simply the woman he had been pushed into marrying because of her one stupid mistake. Someone he felt more for than just a burning sexual desire.

'Come on then.'

Folding his hand around hers, Cesare hoisted her to her feet. And that desire was there like an electrical current as it was every time they touched. It was the reason she had hesitated over taking his hand because it seared across her skin like a blazing brand, frankly terrifying in its intensity. It made her feel out of control and adrift on a storm-tossed sea. She wasn't the person she had thought she was. She didn't recognise the person she became when Cesare touched her.

And clearly Cesare felt it too. It was there in the darkness of his eyes when he looked at her. In the sudden tension of his long body, the swift inhalation of breath that spoke of a swift, shaken reaction to her closeness.

'Cesare…!'

His name was wrenched from her and she put out an unsteady hand, clutching at his arm for support as the world suddenly swung round her, the horizon seeming to tilt once, sharply, then straighten up again. Megan closed her eyes hastily and concentrated on getting her balance back.

'Are you okay? What is it?'

'I'm fine.'

The moment, whatever it had been, had passed, the dizziness receding and everything was back to normal again.

'What happened?'

Was she deceiving herself or was that real concern in Cesare's deep eyes?

'I just felt a bit fuzzy there for a minute. I must have stood up too quickly.'

'Or had too much sun,' Cesare growled disapprovingly. 'With your colouring you really should take more care.'

'I'm fine—honest!'

Megan shifted uncomfortably from one foot to another under the fierce scrutiny he subjected her to. She was painfully aware of the way that the one small awkwardness in what had otherwise been a contented, peaceful sort of day, had changed the mood dramatically.

'Cesare, please don't bother about it!'

But he didn't release her hand even though she was upright and standing at his side. Instead, he drew her close, slid his fingers up along the smooth line of her arm and neck and under her chin, lifting her face to meet his.

'You look a little flushed,' he said, touching a gentle hand to her cheek. 'I should have known better than to keep you out here so long.'

But he hadn't even noticed the time passing, he admitted to himself. The hours had passed in a blink, like so many seconds. There had been a special magic in seeing his old boyhood haunt through her eyes, making him look at it afresh. They had gone swimming as he had always done when he had come here, explored the secret hiding places in the caves where he had often gone to be alone and think when things got on top of him.

'It's no wonder you were dizzy. We'd better get you home so you can get out of the sun and rest.'

He had come here when her father had forced that promise out of him, he remembered as they made their way up
the steep cliff path away from the beach. When Tom had
insisted that he waited, not saying a word, until Megan had
grown up. He hadn't wanted to wait. He'd wanted to tell
her how he felt straight away; couldn't bear the thought of
waiting another five, six years until he could even kiss her.
But at the same time, he'd understood just what was going
through Tom's mind.

Tom had wanted freedom for his daughter. He'd wanted
her to have a chance to grow up and mature, to know her
own mind, before she was asked to commit herself to the
possibility of marriage to anyone. But in the end, if he only
knew it, exactly what Megan's father had feared had come
true. Her so-called freedom had resulted in the painful affair
with Rowell, the mistaken suspicion that she was pregnant.
Which in turn had pushed them both into a hurried wedding
that she would never have wanted had circumstances been
different.

And he had lost his chance to court her in the way he
had wanted.

As always, when he thought of Gary Rowell, a red cloud
of jealousy hazed his mind, blurring his thoughts. He had
never even seen the man and yet he hated him savagely.

'What does Rowell look like?'

It was obviously the last question she had expected and
she paused, slightly further up the path, looking down at
him in bewilderment.

'Why on earth do you want to know?'

'Just curious.'

He obviously hadn't quite hit the casual note he had
aimed for. Something had jarred, making her frown suddenly.

'Why?'

'I wondered what you saw in him.'

What she saw in him! Now how did she answer that? Megan asked herself. And why this question? Why now?

If she had seen it coming, then she might have been better prepared for it, but there was no way she could have anticipated it. It had come right out of the blue, knocking her mentally off balance in a second. And she had no idea at all how to answer it.

CHAPTER ELEVEN

SHE didn't *want* to answer it. Perhaps she could get away with dodging it completely.

'Nothing much...' she muttered, turning and trudging up the path again.

She hadn't really thought that she would get away with it, and she was right. Cesare came after her at speed, his longer legs covering the ground much more quickly than she could manage. He caught her up, just as she reached the flatter ground at the top of the cliff, taking hold of her arm and whirling her round to face him.

'And what the hell does "nothing much" mean?'

The edge of the cliff was uncomfortably close and Megan found that even the slightest glance down towards the beach and the waves crashing against it made her feel uncomfortable again, the dizziness threatening her ability to think clearly. In her haste to get safely back onto secure ground, she snatched her arm from Cesare's grasp and marched towards where the car was parked. Of course he came after her, as she had known he would.

'I don't think that's any of your business!'

'I'm making it my business! Megan—!'

He'd caught her up once again, this time clamping both his hands down on her shoulders so that she was forced to a halt, unable to shake off his much greater strength.

'Are you telling me that you went to bed—gave your virginity to a man you thought was "nothing much"?'

Embarrassment combined with various other unpleasant forms of mental discomfort to make it impossible to think

straight. She only knew she desperately wanted to get
Cesare off this decidedly distressing topic, but she couldn't
think of any way to do it.

Perhaps attack really was the better form of defence?

'What's the matter, Cesare? What's really bugging you?
Is it the fact that it was Gary who—who—deflowered me
and you didn't? Is that what you would have preferred? A
virgin bride who was truly entitled to the white dress she
wore when she trotted up the aisle to you on your wedding
day? Someone who hadn't known any other man's touch
so that she couldn't compare you with her previous lover
when you got her into bed?'

'Don't be bloody stupid! I don't give a damn about that!'

Cesare dismissed her furious accusation with an impe-
rious wave of one powerful hand.

'For one thing, this is the twenty-first century. I may be
Sicilian, but I am not so hypocritical as to think that men
can enjoy sexual freedom while women have to stay at
home, preserving their modesty until they have the sanctity
of marriage to liberate them.'

'Then—'

'And for another…'

Cesare cut across her attempt at an interjection, tossing
back his proud head and looking straight down his aristo-
cratic nose at her.

'I know I need have no fears at all where any comparisons between my performance in bed and Rowell's are concerned. If I was any less the lover he was then you could
not respond to me as you do!'

'I—'

'I know women, *carina*. I know when they are aroused—
when they come alive in my arms. I know when they are
feeling pleasure, when they are out of their minds with
delight—and I know that you find that delight in my bed.

I know it, and because of this I am sure that if you did make any comparisons, then it was your former lover who would come off the worst—not me!'

'Why—you…!'

It was all that Megan could manage. She was totally dumbfounded by his egotistical declaration, knocked sideways by the supreme confidence of it all. The fact that every word of it was true only made matters worse.

'You arrogant swine!'

Her furious insult had no effect on him. Instead it just bounced off his conceited hide, leaving him impervious to her anger.

'Arrogant, maybe!' he retorted. 'But at least I am also honest—or are you going to try and deny the truth of what I said?'

'I'm not going to confirm or deny anything!'

Either way it would stick in her throat. If she tried to lie and say that he wasn't the lover he thought, that he didn't turn her on at all, that she was just pretending to respond to him in bed, he would see straight through the pretence, and despise her for even trying it. And she was damned if she was going to increase his already overly-swelled ego by admitting that from the moment he had first kissed her she had never been able to think of any other man at all.

'I'm not even going to honour your outrageous statement by bothering to answer it. It strikes me that you're already big-headed enough as it is!'

'Which, roughly translated, means that you are too afraid to come right out and say that it's the truth.'

'I'm not *afraid* to do anything!'

The fact that that was exactly how she felt damaged her composure even more.

'I'd tell you if I wanted to.'

'Of course.'

Cesare's smile only incensed her further, destroying the little that remained of her fraying hold on her temper.

'All right! You want the *truth*?' she flung at him, completely losing her grip on her tongue. 'You want to know what Gary looked like—well, the honest truth is that he was a dead ringer for you!— He could have been your twin,' she amended hastily when Cesare frowned, even his fluent English stumped by that particular phrase.

'He...'

If she had seemed stunned earlier, now it was Cesare's turn to look as if he had been slapped hard in the face. He hadn't been prepared for this and he didn't know how to take it.

Gary Rowell had been the dark figure on the edge of his consciousness ever since Megan had first mentioned the other man's name. He was the black cloud that hung over this marriage, one of the barriers that came between Megan and himself, destroying their chances of a real relationship. But that was all he had been—a shadow. He didn't think he was prepared for the rat to become reality—a solid, physical figure with a face and a body he could picture in his thoughts.

And what was the significance of the fact that Rowell looked like him? Were they both of a type that Megan was attracted to? Or, worse, when she responded to him, when she came alive in their bed at night—in his arms—was she doing so because she was imagining that he was her first lover, the man who had broken her heart? The man she had loved and lost.

Pushing his hands into the pockets of his jeans so that Megan wouldn't catch sight of the sudden lack of steadiness that betrayed his inner turmoil, he leaned back against the car with what he hoped was at least a semblance of cool disinterest.

'What exactly does that mean?'

'What it means is that you and Gary Rowell could have been brothers. Tall, black hair, a killer tan, cheekbones you could cut yourself on. He looked even more like you than Gio does, and that's saying something.'

The words just wouldn't be held back now. They came tumbling out of her, jerky and uneven, tripping over themselves in their haste to be spoken. Her tongue was getting tangled up on them but she couldn't stop, had to get it all out, have it all said. Snatching in a deep, raw breath, she went on.

'Why do you think I fell so hard for him in the first place?'

'Why?'

He truly sounded as if he didn't know, but that couldn't be the case. Cesare wasn't that stupid. He had to know what she meant. After the way she had behaved at New Year...

'*Why*? You surely don't need to ask that.'

'I'm asking.'

'But you must know what I mean—what I'm talking about. Gary Rowell was the spitting image of you,' she went on when he shook his head slowly, his eyes taking on a blank, opaque look. 'Probably your double. That's why I was attracted to him in the first place. It was...'

Suddenly realising the dangerous path her words were taking, she changed tack hastily. Letting Cesare know that he had broken her heart at that party, and that it had been because she was so hopelessly in love with him that she had been so vulnerable to Gary's practised seduction techniques, was telling him far too much than was wise.

'I had this almighty crush on you for a couple of years, as a result of which I acted very stupidly at New Year—

flinging myself into your arms and practically saying "Take me, I'm yours".'

'That is exactly what you said, as I recall,' Cesare murmured, earning himself a blazing glare from those burning green eyes.

'Well, you made your feelings very, very clear on that matter—and it *hurt*! So when Gary showed he was interested—more than interested—naturally I saw it as a way of healing that hurt…'

'So now you're saying it's *my* fault you ended up with Rowell? That you ended up pregnant…'

'Except that I didn't end up pregnant after all, so it's not a problem.'

She tried for flippancy, missed it by a mile. The way his face darkened, the deep frown that drew his brows together told her that. And suddenly a cold, creeping sensation slid over her skin, bringing with it a new fear, one she pushed aside quickly, too afraid to face it.

'It was all just a stupid mistake.'

'It might not have been.'

Had he really hurt her that badly? He knew he had been more forceful than he had ever intended, driven to the edge of desperation by the innocent temptation she had offered him, but he had never meant to drive her to *that*! Had he really damaged her self-esteem so that she had flung herself into the arms of the first man who offered?

'Yes, well, now you know that even if I *had* been, it would have looked enough like you for it not to matter. No one would ever have guessed that the poor little thing wasn't yours, that—'

'That didn't matter to me and you damn well know it! I

didn't marry you because you were pregnant—or thought you might be. That had nothing to do with it.'

'No, of course it didn't,' Megan flung at him the bitter taste of pain on her tongue. A pain far worse than the one she had endured with his rejection of her at the New Year.

She had thought that she had been through the worst it was possible to feel then, in those moments after his rejection of her. Now she knew that compared to the agony of soul she had experienced since, it had barely hurt at all.

'We both know why you married me. And if I was ever in any doubt, you spelled it out in words of one syllable. You wanted me in your bed. That was your primary motivation—the one thing that really drove you. You wanted me in your bed and you thought that offering me marriage would get me there.'

Deny it! She begged him miserably in her thoughts. Please, please deny it! Tell me that that wasn't the real reason. That it was just a mask, carefully assumed to cover up the real reason. Oh, I don't need you to tell me that you love me—I won't ask for that. But please, please tell me it wasn't *just* sex!

The silence that had greeted her bitter accusation dragged on and on, until she was ready to scream in pain and frustration. At long last Cesare straightened up, raked one bronzed hand through the black sleekness of his hair, and expelled his breath in a deep, deep sigh.

'Yes,' he said slowly, his voice lacking any emotion whatsoever. 'You're right. That was about it.'

Megan managed a smile that was stiff and tight, lacking in any sort of warmth.

'So now we both know where we stand, don't we? I married you because I was desperate—trapped by a pregnancy that if I'd only waited a week or so I would have discovered never existed. And you married me because you couldn't get into my bed any other way. If you ask me, we're pretty well matched.'

'Yeah,' Cesare muttered bleakly. 'I think I'd agree with that. I'd say we were just about perfect for each other.'

'So what do we do now?'

Cesare lifted his broad shoulders in a shrug that he knew must seem dismissive, coolly indifferent, but he was beyond caring how he looked. What was there left for them to do when they had just, mentally at least, torn each other to pieces? She had told him bluntly that she felt trapped in this marriage, forced into it by the mistaken belief she was pregnant and, in return, lashing out like a wounded animal, he had confirmed her very worst fears of his own motives.

But what the hell had he been supposed to do? Tell the woman who had just described their marriage as a trap that in fact he was crazily in love with her? Let her know that she was his once in a lifetime love, just as Lucia had been Gio's? She would probably have laughed in his face if he had. Told him just what he could do with his love—a love she clearly wanted nothing to do with.

'I don't see that there's anything we can do. Nothing has changed after all. We just know rather more clearly exactly where we stand. So I suppose we might as well go home and continue as before.'

'Home.'

The emotive word was positively the last straw for Megan. Coming on top of everything else, it seemed to split her mind apart. One half hated Cesare with all her soul, loathing him for the way he had treated her, for marrying her solely out of lust, callously manipulating the desperate situation in which she'd found herself for his own selfish ends.

But the other half, the weak, foolish, gullible half, still clung desperately to the love she had always had for him. The love she had dreamed of having returned only to see those dreams shattered and trampled under his uncaring feet.

'*Home*! Do you mean back to the villa?'

'Yes, of course I do. Where else would we go?'

'Oh, it wasn't *where* we went that bothered me!' Once more Megan took refuge in sarcasm, hiding her pain under the cynical words. 'It was what you called it I didn't like.'

'What…'

'We'll go *home*, you said, when you know perfectly well that the villa isn't a home to me at all! It might be *your* home—but to me it's just a place that I live in. It's the place where I eat, where I sleep, where I have sex with my husband because he bought the rights to my body with this ring…'

Wildly she brandished her left hand in the air, waving it right in Cesare's closed, shuttered face.

'But please don't call it my home! It's the house—your villa—my prison—but it really isn't any sort of *home* of mine!'

She'd overstepped the mark, she knew. Said too much, expressed it too forcefully. Her only excuse was that she had been lashing out in her pain. She had been hurting so badly that she had wanted someone else—Cesare preferably—to share her distress.

But he looked anything but hurt. He just looked furious. His expression was dangerous, violent emotion ruthlessly reined in, but fretting at the bit, threatening to break free at any moment. The vicious golden fires that flared in his eyes terrified her so that she took a hasty step backwards, fighting to get a grip on herself and her stupid, stupid temper.

But when he spoke, it was cold and clipped and utterly precise, stunning her with the rigid control that was in such contrast to what she could read in his face.

'Then in that case, *amante*…'

The deliberate, biting cynicism of his tone darkened the term of affection, turning it into something that was the exact opposite.

'If you'll just get into the car, then I'll take you back to your prison at once.'

He even held the car door open for her, waiting as she flounced past, refusing even to glance in his direction for fear she would break down completely. But then just as she was about to lower herself into the passenger seat he caught hold of her arm, making her glance up at him in shock.

'Just one more question,' he growled, forcing the words from between clenched teeth. 'This ''almighty crush'' you had on me once. Am I to take it that you're well and truly over it now?'

He actually sounded as if it mattered, Megan thought for a moment as if… But then of course she realised just why that was. When he had just told her that her body was all he wanted, that he didn't love her at all, then the last thing he wanted was the pressure of thinking she had fallen in love with him. Well, at least she could convince him on that score.

'Oh yes,' she said as airily as she could manage, praying that it sounded convincing 'I got over that a long time ago.

It was one of those silly, schoolgirl things. I've done a lot of growing up since then.'

She knew she'd succeeded when he was silent for a long, long moment. And in that moment he subjected her to the sort of cold-eyed, unfriendly scrutiny that one might turn on a disgusting slug, or a maggot that had been found in the middle of a delicious meal.

'Yes,' he said slowly. 'You certainly have. And I have to admit that I preferred the other—the younger Megan.'

'Well, I'm sorry—but that Megan doesn't exist any more.'

'I can see that. You've grown up all right Megan. I waited a long time for that. It's just a pity that I don't happen to like what you've become.'

CHAPTER TWELVE

IT WAS three weeks since the day of the picnic.

Three weeks in which the first creeping suggestion of a doubt that she had known on that day had turned into rather more than that. Three weeks during which she had waited and watched and worried and prayed—but all to no avail it seemed. The doubt had turned into a worry, the worry to a fear, the fear to a possibility. And this morning that possibility had become something much, much stronger. It had become a definite.

But this time there was no chance that she had made a mistake. This time she wasn't going to take the risk of an over the counter test. She wouldn't trust it one way or the other, she knew. And this time she had to be certain.

She was certain all right.

She was as certain as it was possible to be. She had confided in Gio, and Gio had taken her to a doctor in Palermo. The doctor had done the requisite tests. And he had come back with the answer. And the answer left no room for doubt—or for hope.

She was pregnant with Cesare's child.

A baby that had almost certainly been conceived on that long, passionate night, the first time ever they had made love. A baby that had now been growing secretly inside her for almost eight weeks. A baby that was real, solid fact, not the delusion she had believed herself to be pregnant with before.

It didn't seem possible because she had felt none of the symptoms that had convinced her she was pregnant the first time. Apart from that one brief moment of dizziness that day at the cove and, of course, the later realisation that her period was overdue, and then had missed, she had felt nothing that had made her suspect that this might be a possibility. The baby had come into her life so silently and secretly that it had never crossed her mind it might be there.

'So when are you going to tell Cesare he's going to be a father?' Gio had asked. He hadn't needed to be told that the results of the tests had been positive. He'd seen it in her face as soon as she walked out of the doctor's surgery. She'd sworn him to secrecy until she had decided what to do.

And that was the problem that fretted at her mind every waking moment. It was there in her thoughts as soon as she stirred. It was the last thing she remembered before she went to sleep.

When *was* she going to tell Cesare?

How was she going to tell Cesare?

And what was going to be his reaction when he learned the truth?

From the moment when they had returned from the cove on the day of the picnic, she had expected Cesare to revert to what she called the 'silent mode'. That he would become once again the apparently totally occupied businessman who was out all hours, only ever returning to the villa to sleep and change his clothes.

She couldn't have been more wrong.

Cesare had never been so present in her life. He was there all the time, spending long days with her, taking her places, visiting his family, showing her the island. They had even had long weekends on the mainland, staying in Rome and Naples, and she had only to express an interest in something and it was provided for her.

It was the nights that were different. And the trouble was

that she couldn't quite put her finger on what had changed. The long, hotly sensual nights that they had shared in the first weeks of their marriage now were every bit as long and hot and sensual, but there was a whole new tone about them.

Or, rather, there was something missing from them.

'What are you doing sitting all alone in the dark?'

Cesare's voice sounding so suddenly behind her, made her start nervously, swinging round to face him.

'I—I was enjoying the cool of the evening—the silence,' she managed, grateful for the gathering shadows of the dusk that hid the finer details of her face from him. Her knowledge of the baby was still so new, so raw, that she feared some sign of it might show in her face, revealing more than she was ready to share. 'It made me think of being at home—in my father's garden.'

'And would you like to be at home?'

The question came sharply, too sharply, almost in the same second that he flicked the switch that brought the lights on, making her blink blindly in the sudden brilliance.

'Would you?'

'I'd like to see my father,' she said cautiously, not at all sure where this line of questioning was leading. 'After all, it's been a couple of months now and I—I'd like to see how he is.'

She'd be able to tell him he was going to be a grandfather too. Her father would be delighted at the prospect, she knew. But first she had to find some way of telling the baby's father.

'You spoke to him only the other night.'

'But that was on the phone. It's not the same as actually speaking to someone face to face. Voices can be deceptive.'

'Your father's fine. Better than he has been for ages.'

'Yes, but I need to see for myself.'

'Do you think I wouldn't tell you if I thought you had anything to worry about? Or is it that you don't believe his problems have been sorted out? That I—'

'Of course I believe that you cleared up his debts, paid off all his creditors. You said you would and you've always been a man of your word. It isn't that that's bothering me.'

'Then what is it?'

But that was a question she wasn't yet ready to answer. She tried to force herself to meet his narrow-eyed gaze, but was painfully aware of the way that her own eyes couldn't quite hold steady. She was too aware of the secret she had to hide; too afraid of his possible reaction to it.

'I just want to see my father. Is there anything so very wrong with that?'

'Nothing. As long as that is what you want to do.'

'Of course it is! Cesare, what's wrong with you tonight?'

'Nothing…'

'Nothing? You can't expect me to believe that.'

'No?'

For a moment he studied her, scrutinising every inch of her face with an intensity that made her feel incredibly vulnerable.

'It's just that I've been wondering when this was going to come.'

'When this…?'

But Cesare had walked away from her, heading in the direction of the kitchen, and if she wanted to hear what he had to say, she had to follow him.

'When what was going to come?'

He was opening a bottle of wine, concentrating on the task as if it was something that needed a degree in rocket science. Megan had the strong suspicion that he was making her wait for his answer and she forced herself to bite her tongue and keep silent until the cork slid out of the bottle with a distinct pop.

'This "I want to go home" business.'

'I want to see my father—what's wrong with that?'

The rich red wine swirled into the beautiful crystal glass, Cesare's attention fixed firmly on the way he was pouring it.

'Your home is here—with me,' he stated coldly, not looking up for a second. 'Do you want a drink?'

'Ye—I mean no thanks,' Megan amended hastily, remembering her condition. 'Cesare, what are you talking about? Are you telling me I can't go home?'

She wished he would stop the pantomime with the wine, her teeth snapping together, her foot tapping impatiently on the tiled floor as he inhaled the bouquet, sipped, savoured the flavour for a moment before swallowing appreciatively.

'Would it matter if I did?'

'Of course it would matter! I want to see my father! You can't keep me apart from him—can't say I...'

'Why not? After all, he did that to me.'

Dannazione! Cesare cursed the lapse in attention that had pushed him into the slip of the tongue, giving away far too much. He must be tired, not concentrating properly or he wouldn't have let that out.

But his mind wasn't fully on what he was saying. He was too busy watching Megan, trying to assess her mood, wondering if she knew.

And of course she noticed, pounced on the revealing hint he had foolishly given her.

'Did what to you?'

'Nothing. It doesn't matter. Megan, I don't want to talk about it.'

'But I do! He did what to you? Are you talking about my father?'

'All right, yes! I'm talking about your father!'

But thinking about Gary Rowell.

And that was the problem. He hadn't been able to think straight, concentrate on anything at all ever since he had learned that Rowell was in England, in London—and that he had been looking for Megan. Tom Ellis had let the fact slip in a phone call that afternoon.

Of course Megan's father didn't know anything about his daughter's past experience with Signor Gary Love-rat Rowell. And so, not even suspecting the way the other man had seduced his daughter and then tossed her aside like a used towel, he hadn't seen any reason not to pass on the news that 'a friend of Megan's from university' had called round and was looking for her 'to catch up on old times'.

And if he had passed that news on to his son-in-law, then surely he would also have told Megan about it?

'And what is my father supposed to have done?'

Cesare had been heading back to the sitting-room but now he paused in the marble-floored hallway, swinging round to face her, the glass of wine in his hand seeming almost like some sort of delicate barrier between them.

'Not supposed to have done, Megan,' he said sharply. 'It's what he *has* done.'

'And that is?'

He almost told her. He opened his mouth to speak, then abruptly closed it again, shaking his dark head firmly.

'No.'

'No? Cesare you can't do this!'

He had moved on again, heading for the lounge where he flung himself down in one of the big black leather armchairs, taking a deep swallow of his drink as he did so.

'You have to tell me!'

'Have to?'

The ebony eyes sparked with fire, warning her that this

was quite the wrong approach. One didn't tell Cesare Santorino that he *had* to do anything, not if you wanted to avoid an explosion to equal a volcanic eruption.

'Please tell me,' she amended carefully, lowering her tone by a full octave so that it was suddenly a husky, enticing whisper. And she came to perch on the arm of his chair, curling her long legs up under her.

Did she know what she did to him when she came close like that? Cesare wondered. Did she know how the warm scent of her body, the sweet flowery perfume she wore, coiled around his senses, bringing them to sharp, stinging life immediately?

What was he thinking? Of course she did! Of course she knew the effect she had on him. Just as she knew that the sight of her long slim body in the tight blue jeans and the breast-hugging white cotton T-shirt had set his pulse throbbing from the moment he had entered the room. She knew it and she was using it deliberately to get what she wanted.

'Please...'

One slender-fingered hand rested on his knee, smoothed the fine material of his trousers softly, making his throat dry instantly.

'Cesare... You said my father kept you apart from—from me? Is that what you mean he did?'

His sigh hissed out in a sound that was a blend of exasperation and resignation.

'You're not going to let this drop are you?'

'No. And if it's about me then I have a right to know. If you don't tell me then I shall get right on the phone and ask my father.'

Her smile was mischievous; wicked little kitten with the cream in its sights and no intention of letting it go.

'And I can be very persistent—so you might as well give in now.'

'Okay!'

Cesare decided to surrender. The truth was that he was tired. He was tired of secrets, of hiding things from her. Perhaps if she knew what had really happened.

'Okay. You'll probably find out some time anyway. It might as well be now.'

Megan had no idea what she was expecting, but whatever it was, it was certainly not what she heard. From the moment Cesare told her that he had spoken to her father, she listened wide-eyed, unable to believe a word he said.

'You—you fancied me *then*?' she managed, still finding it hard to take in.

She was remembering something he had said to her a long time ago, a lifetime it seemed. On the night he had come to the house and found her alone and frightened.

'I've never been able to ignore you,' he had said. 'Not from the moment you bounced into my life as a pretty thirteen-year-old, the first time I ever visited this house. I couldn't take my eyes off you then, and I've never been able to since.'

'Not as a thirteen-year-old, obviously!' Cesare was quick to point out. 'Though even then you were a delight. But from the time you were sixteen—yes.'

'And my father made you promise to wait?'

'I gave him my word. I understood what he was trying to do. You see, I knew what he'd been through with your mother—the way he'd tried everything he could to keep her. He spent a fortune on her, bought her anything and everything she wanted. He really thought that would make her stay. But she went anyway, and when she divorced him…'

Painfully aware of the fact that this was her mother he was talking about, he glanced sharply at Megan's face, seeing the sadness that clouded her eyes.

'I'm sorry...' he began but she shook her head fiercely.

'Don't worry about it!' she told him. 'And please don't think I have any delusions about my mother. She walked out on me when I was a child—and I know she treated Dad very badly.'

'She sued for half of everything he possessed. That was the start of his money troubles—he never recovered from the expense of that divorce. And the truth was that his heart wasn't in it after he lost his wife. He let the business get badly run-down, until in the end no one could save it. The only thing I could do was to buy him out—at much more than it was worth—and then write the loss off.'

'It must have cost you a fortune. I hope it was worth it.'

Caught off guard, Cesare couldn't quite hide his surprise.

'You did that for me,' she explained. 'To get me to marry you. I hope I was worth the expense.'

'Worth it?'

Leaning forward, Cesare slammed his glass down on a nearby coffee-table with a lack of care that showed no respect at all for the delicate crystal.

'How could you be anything else?'

The next moment his arms were round her waist, pulling her down onto his lap. His hand went under her chin, lifting her face up to his and his mouth took hers in a kiss that was positively sinful with its promise of heated passion and deep, deep sensuality. She longed to give in to that sensuality, lose herself in the desire that was stirring her blood so hotly, but she knew that that was what she had done all through their marriage and now she needed more.

'I wanted you all my life it seemed. I tried to distract myself with other women, but it didn't work. You were always there—in my blood it seemed—a hunger I could never assuage.'

Wanted, a sad little voice repeated inside Megan's

thoughts. *A hunger. In my blood.* Words of sexual desire. Of passion that she knew he felt. But where were the words she truly needed? Where was the love? The deep, deep caring that would see them through a lifetime together? Them, and this baby. Because she had another life to think about now.

Without those deeper feelings, she was little more than a slave. Bought and paid for with the clearing of her father's debts.

'And so when you thought I was pregnant, it all worked out so well for you. You had the perfect opportunity to manoeuvre me into marriage, so as to get what you wanted. And you threw in helping my father as an added sweetener so that I wouldn't be able to resist.'

Green eyes blazed into brown and to her horror she saw there the shadow of something that twisted in her soul. Guilt? Embarrassment? At what he had done, or simply at being found out?

'No wonder you understood my father's mistakes, Cesare.'

With a rough movement that tore at her heart more than her body, she wrenched herself free from his arms and scrambled inelegantly to the floor. As soon as her feet touched the ground she took several awkward steps back, away from him. She needed to put a distance between them, both mentally and physically so that she could think.

'You're making exactly the same ones—following in his footsteps right up to the trying to buy me and my affections. Well, I'll tell you straight, *mio marito*. It isn't going to work! You can't buy people! You can't keep them with you if they don't want to be there. You can't *bribe* people to love you!'

Now, fight back—*please*! With all the strength of her mind, she tried to will him to argue, to tell her it wasn't so. All she wanted—needed—to hear was that there was more to it than that. That he felt more for her than just wanting to have her in his bed.

He didn't even have to say the word love. If she had to, she would wait for that. If only he would give her *something*. Something to hold on to.

He didn't.

Instead he kept her waiting. His silence was shocking, bewildering, frightening. He let it drag on and on, stretching her nerves to breaking-point, twisting in her soul, making each beat of her heart seem endless, agonising.

And all the time he simply watched her. Heavy, concealing lids hooding his dark eyes, his jaw set and tight, his expression blank and unreadable.

More silence.

And then at last he moved. So suddenly and unexpectedly that she jumped back, startled, as he put both his hands on the arms of his chair and pushed himself to his feet.

He walked away from her, pacing the floor as he had done on the night in the library, making her think once again of the restless prowling of a hunting cat. Then, just as she was about to beg him to stop, to please speak to her, say something, anything, he swung back to face her.

And immediately she wished he hadn't. There was no light in his face, nothing that was soft or gentle or warm. There was only withdrawal and distance, and cold—a cold so deep and intense that even from this distance it chilled her blood and made her shiver fearfully.

'Tell me something,' he said and the quiet, almost conversational level of his voice made her head spin in disbelief.

He might have been talking about the weather forecast, or the price of fish. Anything other than something so fundamental to the future of their relationship that she knew she could never go on without it.

'The way you talked about living here—that day we went to the cove...'

'When I described being here as like being in a prison?'

His nod was so brief as to be almost non-existent.

'Did you mean it?'

There was only one way she could answer that. She had come this far; she couldn't back down now. It was all or nothing. Her whole future and that of her baby, staked on what happened right here and now.

'Yes.'

To be in his life and not have his love was like being in a terrible hell-hole of a prison. To love him as she did and know that he only wanted her for sex, for the completely unemotional gratification of a very basic physical appetite, was like the worst form of torture anyone could devise.

And the worst thing was that she adored her persecutor.

'Yes, I did. I do.'

It was the answer Cesare had been dreading. The answer that told him he had failed completely. He had used up all his ideas, and he had no idea at all what to put in their place.

Because the truth was that he was guilty as charged. He had made every one of the same mistakes as her father. He had tried to buy her affection. He had thought that if he could only get her married to him; if he could only keep her in the arrangement long enough, then she must inevitably come round. That if they spent long enough together, she would finally, eventually, fall in love with him and...

And what? They could live happily ever after?

He almost laughed aloud at the thought but then a swift glance into Megan's face, seeing the distress in her eyes stopped him dead. Every last trace of humour, even the black, grimly cynical amusement that had just twisted in his gut, fled, leaving him icy cold and fatalistically resolved.

And scared out of his life.

He had come hard up against the one answer—the only answer—he could think of. He might have followed in Tom's footsteps, compounding all the older man's mistakes, to get this far, but at least he could learn the lesson his father-in-law had never understood. He could stop everything now, before it got any worse. He could accept the inevitable. And it was inevitable that Megan was never going to love him.

He had to accept that—and let her go. If he didn't, then she was going to end up hating him as her mother had hated her father. And that he couldn't bear.

So he had to stop this now. Even if it killed him to do it.

Drawing a deep, rawly painful breath, he forced himself to speak.

'Okay then, you don't have to suffer any more. You can go.'

'What?'

It was the last thing Megan had been expecting, and because of that she couldn't believe she had heard right. Her head reeled in shock, her thoughts spinning.

'What did you say? I don't understand.'

'It's quite simple. You said that living here was like being in prison. Well, I'm putting that right. I'm taking off the shackles, unlocking the door...'

To Megan's horror he actually marched into the hallway, wrenching open the big front door, letting in the soft evening breeze, the low, distant sound of the sea.

'You can go—walk—anytime you want. This marriage was a mistake right from the very start. I can't give you what you want and quite frankly the appeal of what I was getting from you had already started to fade.'

Not the physical desire, he admitted. But sex without emotion—without love—was not what he wanted. In fact it had become its own form of torture to him, growing more disturbing with every day.

It wasn't that the passion was waning. That was still there. Always would be. He doubted if anything could ever take that from him. In fact, the worst thing about this moment—this terrible, appalling, hateful moment—was the way that even as he had walked past her his body had been responding to the tug of hers.

Foolishly, weakly, he had gone too close to her, and his arm had brushed her. Just his arm, but everything that was masculine in him had leapt in excitement, the ache of hungry need adding to and aggravating the other, emotional agony he was enduring.

And that made it impossible to think straight. To try and couch his feelings in reasonable words. To say what he had to say clearly but gently.

'There's nothing else to understand. I'm ending it. A clean break—finish—here and now. I'll start divorce proceedings first thing in the morning. Don't look at me like that! I'm giving you what you wanted! I'm setting you free. Just go!'

Please go! Please leave now, before I say something so weak, so foolish that you'll despise me for ever.

But still she hesitated, dragging out the moment, the pain, until it was more than he could bear.

'But...I can't go...I...I think I might be pregnant.'

And that was just too much. It was the final, the destructive straw on the camel's back. And just like that one burden too many, it broke him completely, shattering his thought-processes into a million, myriad pieces.

'Oh no, lady! No way! You caught me that way before. I won't put my head in the noose a second time! Not even for you.'

And before Megan could reach him; before she could catch his arm, restrain him, try to get him to listen, he had gone. Walking out of the door and out of her life. And she had no idea at all how—or if—she could ever get him back.

CHAPTER THIRTEEN

'OH, CESARE, *fratello mio.* You have to be the world's greatest fool—or at least the worst one that I know!'

His brother Gio's voice sounded in Cesare's head as he brought the car to a halt outside the villa and switched off the engine.

'I thought you told me that you loved this woman!'

'I do!' Cesare had told him. 'I adore her! I love her more than life itself! But I can't live with her!'

'And why not?'

'Because it would kill me to live with her and know that she can never love me.'

'And who told you this? Did Megan? Did you ever ask her? And did you ever tell her how you feel?'

He hadn't waited for an answer. He'd read it in his brother's face and he flung up his hands in a gesture of exasperation and disgust.

'*Madre de Dio*, Cesare—what has happened to your brain? Do you expect the poor girl to read your mind? Let me tell you something...'

And the something he had to say had had Cesare racing for his car, slamming it into gear and heading back to the villa as swiftly as the winding, narrow roads would let him.

But now that he was here he found that his heart was pounding as if he had run a marathon. He wanted this moment to be over so that he would know once and for all where he stood. And he also knew that if he could delay it for ever, then he would.

At least right now he still had a chance either way. But

if he asked her how she felt and the answer was not the one he wanted, then he was done for; his future—the future he hoped for—blocked once and for all and no hope left.

And then there was the problem of the taxi.

It had passed him on the way here—heading away from the villa. And, as it was empty and this road went nowhere else but to his house, then the taxi's passenger had to be still at the villa. Who did Megan know on the island who she could call to come and see her like this?

Some instinct kept his movements careful and quiet as he made his way into the house. He didn't want to alert anyone until he saw just how the land lay. And what he discovered made him thankful he had adopted such a plan, his heart clenching in bitter anger when he saw just who the visitor was.

They were out by the pool at the back of the house, which was why they hadn't heard his car arrive. Megan was beautiful as ever in a long, white dress, short-sleeved and scoop-necked, her glorious hair slightly tousled by the breeze. The man with her he had never seen before in his life, but he didn't need any introductions or explanations to work out just who he was.

'You and Gary Rowell could have been brothers,' Megan had said, and looking through the open patio doors at the man who stood beside his wife, he knew that her description had been totally accurate. If it wasn't for the fact that he had just left Gio in his half-brother's house where he had spent the night after walking out on Megan yesterday, then he would have assumed that that was who this visitor was. But of course there was only one man he could be.

'Rowell!'

The name hissed through his lips as he stepped back hastily, moving out of sight of either of the two people by the pool. He didn't want to be seen until he had worked out just what was going on here.

And what he feared was the worst.

How could Gary Rowell have come to be here, at his villa, unless Megan had let him know where she was? And to do that, she must have known that he was in London and looking for her. There was just enough time for her to have phoned him after their argument last night, told him to get on the first plane out here... And if she had done that, then she must still love him. ·

For a moment he was tempted to leave. But even as he turned he heard Gio's words, harsh and stark inside his head, and knew that he couldn't give in now. Sighing, he turned back again.

Megan was still in shock from Gary's sudden appearance. When she had heard the sound of a car drawing up outside the villa, she had assumed that it was Cesare, coming back at last. And so she had rushed to the door, pulled it open and, at first, she had almost believed that the tall, dark man outside was in fact her husband.

But then she saw the blue of his eyes, heard the voice.

'Hi babe.'

Only one man had ever called her 'babe' in just that drawl. Only one man had ever grinned that 'Aren't you glad to see me?' grin. And that man was someone she had never wanted to see again.

But here he was, large as life, on her doorstep. And the worst thing was that she couldn't tell him to turn right round and go away because, even as she registered just who he was, the taxi driver, obviously paid and dismissed, was heading off down the road far too fast to be called back.

And she couldn't just leave him standing outside, much as she might like to. She had felt obliged to offer him at least a drink and somewhere to sit while he waited for another taxi to take him away again. Which couldn't be soon enough as far as she was concerned. She had spent a long, desperately lonely night waiting for Cesare and she certainly didn't want him to find Gary here when he got back.

He *had* to come back. He couldn't stay away for ever. If nothing else, he had to return to the villa to get some clothes. And so she had waited for him. And waited. And waited. Until at last she had fallen asleep on the settee, sleeping in total exhaustion until just twenty minutes before the taxi had arrived.

'Lovely place, you have here.'

Gary was clearly determined to make conversation.

'It's my husband's house. He and his family are Sicilians.'

'So I heard. I have to admit that I couldn't believe my ears when your father told me you were married and where you lived. But then I heard just *who* you'd married and it all fell into place.'

Megan frowned lightly in confusion.

'I don't know what you mean.'

'Oh, come on, babe, you know exactly what I mean. Cesare Santorino—friend of the family—loaded from what I hear. You've done very nicely for yourself. And you always did have the hots for him.'

Megan bit her lip hard. She'd forgotten how one night, in a foolish attack of honesty, she'd told Gary all about Cesare, and how he'd callously (or so she had thought then) rejected her at the New Year party.

That had been part of her downfall, she remembered bitterly. Gary had been very understanding. Apparently deeply sympathetic. She'd trusted him, fallen into his arms, and he had expertly taken advantage of the situation to get her into his bed.

'I see you rethought your stance on abortion too. Clearly you got rid of it, in spite of all your protestations. Otherwise you'd be showing a lot more by now. Clever girl! I don't suppose your Sicilian would have wanted you if he'd known you were carrying another man's bastard. Where is your lord and master by the way?'

'He—he'll be back any minute.'

She prayed it would be true.

'Gary, exactly what are you doing here?'

'You don't think I just dropped by to say Hi?'

'Quite frankly, no. I don't believe it.'

She didn't believe what she heard next, either. Listening in growing horror to the story Gary poured out, she was forced to wonder what, apart from the resemblance to Cesare, she had ever seen in him. She had known that Gary Rowell was shallow, selfish and totally thoughtless. Now she discovered that he was greedy, mercenary and thoroughly unscrupulous as well.

Judging her on his own immoral terms, he had assumed that she would never have confessed her pregnancy to Cesare. Obviously believing she really had been carrying his child, he had also decided that she must have got rid of it—and that she would be terrified of her new husband finding out. And he was offering to keep quiet about their relationship—for a price.

'Your guy can afford it,' he said, a wave of his hand indicating the luxurious villa, the water of the pool glinting in the morning sunlight. 'And surely you can persuade him to give you what you need—just be extra nice to him in bed and I'm sure he'll come through. And then he won't need to know about our love affair...'

Megan had had enough. She didn't want to hear any more. And she certainly didn't have time or inclination to deliver the truth in anything other than its starkest form.

'He knows,' she said baldly. 'Cesare knows everything. You don't think I could have married him and not been completely honest? He knows all there is to know about you and me! And don't even try to call it a love affair because it was nothing of the sort! There was no *love* between us—never was. I might have been stupid enough to believe that once but not any more! Now I know what love is really like...'

She broke off hastily, interrupted by a savage expletive from the man before her.

'Are you saying...' he snarled, 'that I've come all this way for nothing?'

The expression on his face frightened her and she took a hasty step backwards.

'That's exactly what I'm saying. I want you to go.'

'Why you—!'

She saw what was coming but was unable to stop it. Gary launched himself at her, hand upraised. But he never reached her. There was a blur of movement. A tall, dark figure dressed completely in black emerged from the house at speed and Gary was whirled away from her, his attack swiftly converted into a desperate defence. After the briefest of struggles, he was suddenly thrown backwards, arms whirling ineffectively, until he landed with a heavy splash right in the shallow end of the pool.

Cesare waited a nicely calculated minute until his defeated opponent surfaced again, spluttering inelegantly and spitting water, and then at last he spoke.

'You heard the lady—she wants you to go. Get out of my sight. And in future, if you're wise, you'll leave my wife alone—or you'll have me to answer to.'

Turning on his heel, he held out his hand to Megan and led her firmly into the house, shutting the patio doors securely behind them, and drawing the curtains over them for good measure. Only then did he turn to Megan.

'Are you okay? Did he touch you!? If he did, I'll...'

'I'm okay,' Megan assured him.

'All the same, you'd better sit down.'

He led her to a chair, lowered her into it.

'Can I get you something? A glass of water? Tea?'

'Cesare, I'm *fine*.'

She wished he would just stop fussing. From the moment he had first appeared, springing to her rescue like some action adventure hero, she hadn't been able to get a good look at his face. And she needed to be able to see his face to read his emotions in it. She needed to be able to judge his mood. To try to understand why he was here, and what, apart from the instinctive reaction to protect her from Gary, he felt about her.

'Please, sit down—or at least stay still for a moment.'

He complied with the second request at least. But even when he was still, she couldn't begin to tell what frame of mind he was in. His face was expressionless and unrevealing, his eyes blank and opaque.

'Thank you for your help out there. I was worried...'

'I wouldn't have let him hurt you. If he'd touched you, I'd have torn him limb from limb. But men like that are cowards. They might try and threaten someone weaker than themselves, but they'd never take on a real opponent.'

'You soon sorted him out anyway.'

In spite of, perhaps because of, her uncertainty about Cesare himself and the tension of the moment she found that an attack of nervous giggles was bubbling up inside her, forcing its way out.

'And the look on his face as he hit the water—it was priceless!'

'He should count himself lucky that he got away with a

soaking,' Cesare growled, his expression not lightening in the slightest in response to her laughter. 'If I hadn't been here…'

'But you were.'

Abruptly the giggles vanished, leaving her painfully sober and once more unsure of herself.

'Cesare, *why* are you here?'

For a moment that black glare faltered, then his control slammed back into place.

'Isn't it obvious? You said you were pregnant.'

Any last trace of laughter fled from her mind at his tone. Of course, he was here for the baby. But did that mean he was here for her too? After all, she came along with her child—but were they also together in Cesare's heart?

'But you said you weren't putting your head in that noose again…'

Cesare sighed, pushing a hand through the darkness of his hair.

'I said a lot of stupid things last night, of which that was one. If you're pregnant with my child, of course I'll be there for you.'

And what were the other 'stupid things'? Megan didn't know if she dared ask. Instead, she stuck to practical things.

'Where've you been? I waited up all night and you never came.'

'No. I went to Gio's house. I needed to calm down, get my head straight. I talked to Gio a lot and he said some things that got me thinking.'

Now she had to ask.

'Thinking about what?'

'You and me for one.'

Megan's mouth had gone very dry and nothing she could do would relieve it.

'I think I'd like that glass of water now,' she managed to croak.

But she couldn't wait for him to come back with it and she followed him into the kitchen, a thousand butterflies fluttering in her stomach.

'Is there a you and me to think about, Cesare?' she asked hesitantly.

He didn't answer at first but finished pouring the water then handed the glass to her, ice clinking on the side, and she drank from it gratefully, the cool water easing her parched throat.

'I need to tell you something,' he said, his expression worryingly sombre.

She would never know how she swallowed that last mouthful of water, somehow getting it past the tight knot that had closed her throat. Carefully she put the glass down on the nearest counter.

'What?'

He glanced around at the huge farmhouse kitchen, grimaced slightly, his mouth twisting wryly.

'This isn't exactly the best place for this, but I can't wait any longer. Meggie—how would you feel if I said that I loved you?'

That 'Meggie' had caught her on the raw. It was so long since she had heard him call her by the shortened, affectionate form of her name. Before she had time to think, her eyes had filled with tears and she was blinking hard to hold them back.

Then she realised just what he had finished the question with and she gave up on restraint and let them fall.

'Meggie, *cara*!' Cesare's tone was shocked and bewildered. 'What have I done? I'm sorry. I didn't mean to upset you! I just—'

'Just said the thing I most wanted to hear in all the

world,' Megan put in hastily, her hands going out and closing over his. 'Oh Cesare, did you mean it?'

'Could you doubt it? Yes—*yes* I love you...'

The rest of his words were smothered against his lips as Megan flung herself into his arms and kissed him hard. They were both breathing fast, their hearts thudding loudly by the time they managed to separate again.

Megan's spirits were bubbling, her heart soaring, singing, until she felt it would burst with happiness.

'Do you know how long I've waited for you to say that? How I've dreamed, prayed...'

'But you said that living here with me was like being a prisoner.'

'Being here, with you, *without your love*, was like being in prison,' Megan corrected gently. '*With* your love, I'd never want to be anywhere else.'

'Then I did hear right. What you said to Rowell about love...'

'About knowing what it's really like? Yes, you heard right, my darling. I knew I had never felt anything like love for Gary because deep in my heart you had always been the one. It's just that—that I got a little off track for a while at the beginning of the year.'

She knew that Cesare had understood by the way that his face sobered swiftly.

'After the New Year party. Meggie, I'm so sorry about that. I never meant to hurt you so badly.'

'Ssh.'

She laid her hand across his lips to silence him.

'I know now why you did it. You'd given my father your word. And if the way you kept to that, in spite of everything, shows me how you'll keep our wedding vows, then we're going to have a wonderful, lasting, lifetime of marriage.'

'Oh, I hope so!' Cesare declared fervently. 'I shall need a lifetime to show you how I feel about you.'

He put his feelings into actions, hugging her close and taking her mouth again.

'Cesare,' Megan managed eventually when at last he released her so that she could gasp in a few much-needed breaths. 'What was it that Gio said?'

'When he made me realise what a fool I'd been?'

Cesare reached for her left hand, ran his finger over the shining golden band that he had placed on it a few months before. Then he lifted it to his lips and pressed a lingering kiss on both finger and ring.

'It was quite simple really. He told me that every day since Lucia had died he had never gone to sleep without wishing that he could tell her how much he loved her just one more time. If I needed anything to bring home to me how much time I was wasting, then that was it. I couldn't get here quick enough.'

'You got here just in time,' Megan said and they both knew that she didn't just mean because of Gary Rowell.

'I know.'

Still holding her hand, he looked deep into her eyes.

'Megan, *amante*, will you really stay with me—can we truly start again and have a real marriage as husband and wife?'

'I can think of nothing I would want more.'

Relief flooded his face and the wide, wonderful smile that she loved came back with a vengeance.

'Then I think that at last we're ready...'

'Ready for what?' Megan asked curiously. But he only shook his head, his expression mysterious.

'You'll see. Come with me.'

He led her out of the kitchen and up the stairs. Turning away from the room that had been theirs since they had arrived in Sicily, he took her down the landing to a door at the end. Pulling a key from his pocket, he unlocked the door and pushed it open. Then caught at her arm to hold her back as she moved forward.

'No, wait!'

'Cesare!'

It was a gasp of surprise as he swung her off her feet, carried her into the room.

'*Cesare!*'

If she'd been surprised before, now she was stunned. Staring round her in bewilderment she recognised everything. The bed, the furniture, the curtains. Even the nightdress lay spread out on the downy gold and green quilt.

'It—it's your room—the one in England…' she stammered and saw his dark head nod agreement.

'The one where we should have spent our wedding night if we hadn't been interrupted by events. I had everything brought from England in the hope that this day might arrive.'

Carrying her across the room, he lowered her to the bed and sank down beside her.

'You see, *adorata*,' I never got to have the wedding night I wanted. The one I wanted you to have. I was going to tell you how I felt then.'

'You can tell me now.'

'I can and I will. I can tell you that I love you with every breath that's in my body, with every beat of my heart, and I'll go on loving you until both of them stop. I love you more than life; you are my reason for living, the light that welcomes me into every new day. And if I can start each of those new days by telling you how much I love you then, no matter what the day holds, I will be happy.'

'Oh Cesare!' Megan sighed, reaching for him. But to her astonishment, he stilled her gently.

'But that's not all. Then I was going to take you in my arms and kiss your face…your hair, your eyes…

He suited action to the words, kissing her until her mind was swimming with delight.

'And then?' she sighed.

'And then I was going to take the clothes from your body, kissing every inch of your skin as I uncovered it…'

The breath caught in Megan's throat in delighted anticipation and she lay back, submitting completely to his attentions as he did just that. By the time he had finished she was burning with heat and her pulse was throbbing ferociously.

'And then?' She could barely get it out.

'I was going to caress your breasts, hold them, kiss them, suckle…'

The words were lost as his passion destroyed his restraint, his ability to speak. And Megan too was there with him, moaning her need, the need he had ignited, the need they both shared.

The need to seal their love with this perfect act of union.

And it was perfect. It was slow and gentle and sensuous and giving. And when they both reached the moment of ecstasy together she knew there could be no better beginning to their real married life.

'Sweetheart,' Cesare whispered a long, long time later when some degree of calm had returned, and with it the ability to think. 'Are you really pregnant?'

'Yes, I am. And this time it's real.'

She reached for his hand, laid it on her body.

'This time I had it confirmed. That's where our baby is, my love. That's where he or she is lying safe and secure, growing bigger every day.'

His sigh of contentment seemed to come right from his soul it was so deep and strong.

'So then I think it's time for this…'

And reaching under the pillow, he pulled out the jeweller's box and flipped it open, revealing a stunning ring, a deep-red, heart-shaped ruby surrounded by brilliant diamonds.

'Cesare!' Megan gasped. 'It's wonderful—but what…?'

'It was going to be the last thing I did before we fell asleep,' he told her. 'It's the engagement ring I never had a chance to give you. I was going to give it to you and ask you all over again, and properly this time, if you would do me the very great honour of becoming my wife. And I was going to beg you not to keep me waiting long for an answer.'

He looked deep into the green depths of her eyes as he spoke and he saw her smile start there before it had even touched her mouth.

'I won't,' she whispered, 'I won't keep you waiting a moment longer. And of course, my darling, the answer is yes.'

The world's bestselling romance series.

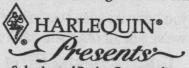

HARLEQUIN® Presents~

Seduction and Passion Guaranteed!

Your dream ticket to the vacation of a lifetime!

Why not relax and allow Harlequin Presents® to whisk you away to stunning international locations with our new miniseries...

FOREIGN AFFAIRS

Where irresistible men and sophisticated women surrender to seduction under the golden sun.

Don't miss this opportunity to experience glamorous lifestyles and exotic settings in:

**Robyn Donald's
THE TEMPTRESS OF TARIKA BAY**
on sale July, #2336

THE FRENCH COUNT'S MISTRESS
by Susan Stephens
on sale August, #2342

THE SPANIARD'S WOMAN
by Diana Hamilton
on sale September, #2346

THE ITALIAN MARRIAGE
by Kathryn Ross
on sale October, #2353

FOREIGN AFFAIRS... A world full of passion!

Pick up a Harlequin Presents® novel and you will enter a world of spine-tingling passion and provocative, tantalizing romance!

Available wherever Harlequin books are sold.

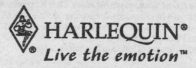

HARLEQUIN®
Live the emotion™

Visit us at www.eHarlequin.com

HPFAMA

If you enjoyed what you just read,
then we've got an offer you can't resist!

Take 2 bestselling
love stories FREE!
Plus get a FREE surprise gift!

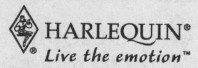

HARLEQUIN®
INTRIGUE®

presents another outstanding installment
in our bestselling series

COLORADO CONFIDENTIAL

By day these agents are cowboys; by night they are
specialized government operatives. Men bound by love,
loyalty and the law—they've vowed to keep their
missions and identities confidential...

August 2003
ROCKY MOUNTAIN MAVERICK
BY GAYLE WILSON

September 2003
SPECIAL AGENT NANNY
BY LINDA O. JOHNSTON

In **October,** look for an exciting short-story collection
featuring *USA TODAY* bestselling author
JASMINE CRESSWELL

November 2003
COVERT COWBOY
BY HARPER ALLEN

December 2003
A WARRIOR'S MISSION
BY RITA HERRON

PLUS
FIND OUT HOW IT ALL BEGAN
with three tie-in books from Harlequin Historicals,
starting January 2004

Available at your favorite retail outlet.

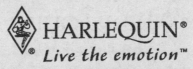

HARLEQUIN®
Live the emotion™

Visit us at www.eHarlequin.com   HICCAST

The world's bestselling romance series.

HARLEQUIN®
Presents

Seduction and Passion Guaranteed!

RED HOT REVENGE

There are times in a man's life...
when only seduction will setttle old scores!

Pick up our exciting new series of revenge-filled romances—
they're recommended and red-hot!

Coming soon:

MISTRESS ON LOAN by Sara Craven
On sale August, #2338

THE MARRIAGE DEBT by Daphne Clair
On sale September, #2347

Available wherever Harlequin books are sold.

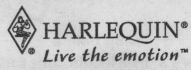

HARLEQUIN®
Live the emotion™

Visit us at www.eHarlequin.com